"We've lost our

He glanced at Kim
fear.

Ahead was a sharp curve and a steep drop. At this speed they'd fly over the edge. Rick had no choice. He rammed into a scrub oak thicket. They fishtailed, then finally slid to a stop, dust enveloping them in a cloud.

"This was no accident," she said.

He crawled beneath the SUV and studied the damage. "You're right. Someone cut the brake line." When he came back out, his jaw was set. "I let my guard down, Kim. I'm sorry."

"I don't understand."

"I'm on the job. I should know better than to get so distracted by you."

"I wouldn't trade a second of what happened between us," she said, holding his gaze. "It drew us closer, and if you allow it, it'll make us even stronger."

It could also get them killed...

Dear Reader,

Aimée always believed in the power of love, and the forty-three year romance we shared kept us together from the moment we met. I was with her when she died in February, just a few weeks after completing *Eagle's Last Stand*. We spent those days side by side—I had her back, and she had my heart. Those hours were precious because we were together, doing what we loved most. There were no regrets. Aimée was at peace, in our own home with her beloved pets, friends and family.

I'm proud to have been the husband, lover, best friend and writing partner of one of the most talented individuals I've ever known. We worked as a team, but it was Aimée who led the way, creating these stories of love, family, loyalty and honor that will live well beyond her life here on earth.

As you read *Eagle's Last Stand*, open your mind to the words, thoughts and feelings that flow from Aimée's heart into your own, and never forget that friendship, love and romance *can* last longer than a lifetime.

In Aimée's own words—"With love we can soar and accomplish anything."

David Thurlo

EAGLE'S LAST STAND

—

AIMÉE THURLO

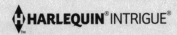

ISBN-13: 978-0-373-74859-4

Eagle's Last Stand

Copyright © 2014 by Aimée and David Thurlo

Printed in U.S.A.

IN MEMORIAM

Aimée Thurlo was an internationally known bestselling author of mystery and romantic suspense novels. She was the winner of a Career Achievement Award from *RT Book Reviews*, a New Mexico Book Award in contemporary fiction and a Willa Cather Award in the same category.

Aimée was born in Havana, Cuba, and lived with her husband and writing partner, David, in Corrales, New Mexico, in a rural neighborhood filled with horses, alpacas, camels and other assorted livestock. David was raised on the Navajo Indian Nation. His background and cultural knowledge inspired many of the Aimée Thurlo stories for Harlequin Intrigue.

We at Harlequin are saddened by the loss of Aimée and collectively send our deepest condolences to David. Aimée was a genuine and lovely woman who we, along with her many fans, will miss greatly.

CAST OF CHARACTERS

Rick Cloud—The former FBI undercover operative had escaped death once before, but now he and his family had become targets. Rick was forced to uncover what really happened to his foster father. He struggled to retain his focus, but was distracted by the intriguing young woman who'd become his partner in the search for the truth.

Kim Nelson—She'd been taking police science courses and working part-time jobs until the explosion took away much more than her uncle's tavern. Her only hope for a future required her to team up with Rick, the cynical, scarred Navajo man who'd stolen her heart the night he'd walked into her life.

Preston Bowman—His Navajo foster brothers and their families had almost died during an event that was supposed to be a homecoming celebration. Preston was a Hartley detective, though, and quickly took control of the investigation. This was a family affair, and the more he learned, the more personal the case became.

Hosteen Silver—For months the six foster brothers believed that the *hataalii* (medicine man) who'd turned their lives around had suddenly become ill, then walked off into the desert to die—as was the custom among traditional Navajos. Yet no body had ever been found. Was he murdered, or was he still alive, hiding out and targeted by a relative of one of his patients?

Angelina Curley—The Navajo woman had been Hosteen Silver's apprentice, until he discovered she was stealing and recording sacred rituals for her own purposes. Angelina was a wealthy businesswoman now, but she made no secret of her hatred for her former mentor and his adopted sons.

Daniel Hawk—Luckily his security company had the resources to investigate and determine who was trying to kill off those closest to him.

Tim McCullough—As a college professor he was required to maintain his credentials, but it was difficult learning the ceremonial secrets of a Navajo medicine man. Just how far would he go to get the information he needed, and at what price?

Nestor Sandoval—It hadn't taken Hosteen Silver long to determine that Nestor lacked the character to become a Navajo healer. As soon as he was turned away, Nestor turned on the old man, a serious mistake that now incurred the wrath of Rick and his five brothers.

Chapter One

He'd wondered what this night would be like, and now he knew. Rick Cloud smiled as he looked around the private dining room his foster brothers and their wives had reserved for his homecoming. For years the Brickhouse Tavern had been one of their favorite watering holes, so it had been the perfect place for the celebration.

Gene Redhouse, the only rancher among the six Navajo men, came up and patted him on the back. "Welcome home," he said, then laughed as he saw their brothers Kyle Goodluck and Daniel Hawk clear away part of the heavy trestle table so they could arm wrestle. "They're at it again."

"Some things never change." Rick's eyes strayed to the pretty hostess as she moved around the room, making sure everyone's glasses were filled and watching over them like a beautiful guardian angel. She was tall and slender, with shoulder-length honey-colored blond hair and beautiful green eyes that didn't seem to miss even the tiniest of details. As he watched, she took away an empty dish of guacamole and replaced it with spicy salsa and blue corn tortilla chips.

"That's Kim Nelson. Do you remember her from high school?"

"I never met her. If I had, I would have remembered," Rick said without hesitation.

"She was a freshman when you were a senior," Gene said. "To hear her talk when we were discussing the plans for tonight, I think she used to have a thing for you. Kyle says it's because you were quarterback, but I fail to see the reasoning. You hand off or throw the ball, take some hits and run the option once in a while. Barely got your jersey dirty most games."

"Jealous, bro?" Rick said, and laughed.

"Nah. I'm the one who ended up with the prize," he said, looking across the room at the pretty brunette watching the match. "Lori's the perfect wife for a cowboy like me."

"You were born to be a rancher," Rick said. "I'm glad you're happy."

As Gene went back to join his wife, Rick found he couldn't take his eyes off Kim. Even the way she moved caught his attention. The woman possessed a presence; a dynamic combo of grace and confidence that kept him searching the dining room for her.

Finally he forced himself to look away. He didn't

need this now. Though he'd never been the ladies' man his brothers thought him to be, he'd never had trouble finding company. Now that his face was marked by a scar that ran across his nose and cheek, a leftover from a deadly knife fight, things would undoubtedly be different.

As Kim worked the room, smiling but definitely staying in the background, he noted the way she'd sometimes glance in his direction. He was about to seek her out when she came over.

"You're the guest of honor tonight, Mr. Cloud. Is there anything special I can get for you?"

"No, I'm good, thanks," he said. She had spectacular green eyes that stayed on his, never shifting for a quick look at his scar. Kim couldn't have missed it, yet she still focused on *him*.

"I'm Kim, the events coordinator here at the Brickhouse."

He shook her hand. "Nice to meet you. And call me Rick."

"Your brothers wanted to make sure every detail of your homecoming was perfect, Rick. That's one of the reasons I stayed to handle things personally. The other, I've got to admit, is because I was curious to see you again. I knew who you were back in high school, but I don't think you ever noticed me," she said with a little smile.

"Definitely my loss."

She smiled. "When Preston Bowman came to

book the restaurant for the private event, my uncle and I knew we had to make this evening super special."

His brother Preston, the lead detective on the Hartley, New Mexico, police department, had a way about him that intimidated most people. "Preston carries that much weight?"

"Actually he does, with me and my uncle, that is."

Something in her tone of voice caught his attention, but before she could say anything more, they heard a loud thump in the kitchen and the rattle of a pot or pan bouncing on the floor.

Kim jumped. "I better go see what happened," she said, excusing herself.

"Wait," he said, reaching for her hand. Something felt off. He took a shallow breath and caught the familiar scent of rotten eggs. It seemed to be growing stronger with each passing second.

"That's a gas leak," he told Kim, then called out to his brothers. "Everyone outside! Quickly."

"It's getting stronger," Daniel said. "Let's go, people!" He pulled his wife, Holly, toward the front door.

Rick's other brother, Paul Grayhorse, got there first but the door refused to budge. "It's locked!" He turned the knob and shoved, but the door didn't open. "No, it's stuck or jammed."

"Force it," Gene shouted. "Kick it open if you have to!"

"I'll check the back," Rick said, turning toward the kitchen.

"I've got to check on my uncle!" Kim rushed past him. She started coughing as she pushed through the double doors to the kitchen. "Uncle Frank? Where are you?"

As Rick caught up to her, they found Frank Nelson lying on the floor beside a long counter, blood oozing from the back of his head.

Kim knelt beside her uncle. "He's unconscious. We have to get him out of here," she cried out.

Out of the corner of his eye, Rick noticed movement. It was a flexible metal gas line against the wall behind the stove. Cut in two, it was fluttering slightly from the outflow of methane. Nearby lay a pair of heavy-duty, red-handled bolt cutters.

"We've got to get out of here before a spark sets off an explosion," Rick yelled. "Help me pull him out the back."

Her eyes narrowed as the foul stink of gas flooded the kitchen, but she didn't panic. Kim took her uncle's arm and Rick the other, and together they dragged Frank toward the rear exit.

Rick then pushed the left half of the double doors hard with his shoulder. It creaked, but only opened a few inches before it stopped with a rattle.

He looked down into the gap between the doors.

"They're chained from the outside," he said, nearly gagging from the strong outflow of methane.

Putting his back into it, Rick pushed even harder. The doors squealed, but held tight.

"We're trapped! Maybe the front door?" Kim looked toward the dining area.

Following her gaze, Rick could see his brothers all leaning into the door. Slowly they forced it open enough to give Erin, Kyle's wife and the smallest of the women, room to slip through the gap.

"We can't wait. I've got to break the doors down." Rick pulled the unconscious man aside, lowered him to the floor and then took a step back. Bracing his arm against his body, he rushed the left door with a yell.

Rick's two hundred and twenty pounds of muscle crashed against the doors. The brass handles broke with a loud snap and the doors flew open. Rick stumbled halfway across the loading dock and crashed into the guard rail before he could stop himself.

Racing back into the kitchen, he reached Frank and Kim, who was down on her knees beside her uncle. Glancing through the kitchen toward his brothers, Rick saw Daniel, the last of the party, just ducking out.

"Time to leave," Rick yelled. He put Frank Nelson over his shoulder and strode quickly down the steps of the loading dock. "Hurry," he added, looking back at Kim.

Kim slipped under the guard rail, jumped off the edge of the platform and met Rick at the bottom of the steps. Just then, Kyle and Preston came around the corner of the Brickhouse, running toward them.

"Get back!" Rick yelled, jogging toward the street with the injured man over his shoulder. "The place can blow any second!"

With Kim beside him, Rick angled left, heading for the corner of the next building over, a former theater turned furniture store. He wanted a solid structure between them and the upcoming blast.

As he reached the sidewalk, he saw his family, en masse, racing across the street in a loose cluster. They had no time to find cover. "On the ground!" he yelled.

Rick dropped to his knees and lowered Frank to the sidewalk. Pulling Kim down and against the wall of the building, he covered her with his body.

Suddenly the earth shook, shaking him back and forth as a massive concussive wave and flash of light swept out into the street. A blinding ball of hot air and flames followed, shooting out of the alley to his left and reaching halfway across the avenue.

The windows on the real-estate office a hundred feet away shattered, raining glass onto the sidewalk. Turning his head slightly, he could see the people he loved, facedown on the far side of the street beside the curb, arms over their heads.

A cascade of falling debris became an ear-shattering hailstorm of bricks and building materials. This went on for several seconds, then began to subside, overwhelmed by the roar and crackle of the resulting fire.

Rick rose to his feet, his mind racing. "You okay?" he asked Kim.

"My uncle… Where is his pulse?" She searched the area around his neck with a trembling hand.

"He's breathing…he's alive. Put pressure on the head wound and I'll call an ambulance," Rick said, turning his back to the wave of heat from the burning building less than twenty-five feet away.

"I called 9-1-1," Preston said, coming up to him. He nodded at the older man on the sidewalk. "Let's get him farther away from the fire in case there's a secondary explosion."

Together he and Rick carried Frank into the recessed doorway of the furniture store. "Did you get a good look around the kitchen?" Preston asked. "What happened in there?"

"It was no accident. The gas line was cut," Rick answered. "I saw bolt cutters nearby. Somebody must have decked Frank, then cut the gas line and slipped out into the alley."

Preston's gaze swept over his brothers, their

wives and the two waiters from the Brickhouse. They'd walked down the street several feet away from the fallen glass and stepped up onto the sidewalk as the first fire truck arrived. "Looks like we're all okay, and that's nothing short of a miracle," he said.

"I'm used to being targeted," Rick said, his voice reflecting the darkness inside him, "but the cartel I dealt with liked keeping things up close and personal. Cutting a gas line and hoping I'd be caught in an explosion just doesn't fit their M.O. My enemies are a lot more direct and efficient."

"Whoever it was didn't just come after you. They came after all of us brothers, and that was a big mistake," Daniel said, coming up beside them.

"Not necessarily," Rick said. Years of undercover work for the FBI, fighting human trafficking, had taught him that control and clear thinking spelled the difference between life and death. Emotions only got in the way. "Others were there, too."

"You mean they were after our wives?" Paul asked incredulously.

"More likely the restaurant staff," Rick said. "If the doors hadn't been blocked, another motive would have been to burn down the business so the owner could collect the insurance."

His gaze drifted back to Kim, who was crouched by her uncle. The bleeding had slowed from what he could see.

"Kim, who's the owner of the Brickhouse?" he asked, going over and placing a gentle hand on her shoulder.

"My uncle Frank is half owner," she said, never taking her eyes off her uncle. "His business partner is Arthur Johnson, but Art would never think of burning down the place or hurting anyone, especially Frank. Those two have been good friends for years, and the Brickhouse has always made money for both of them. You guys are off base on this."

"I'd have to agree with Kim. There's no way this place is losing money. It's always packed," Preston said.

"Gene's grabbed a big wrench from the toolbox in his pickup and he's going to shut off the gas at the meter. That'll help the firemen," Daniel said.

"Meanwhile," Preston suggested, "let's focus on what we know. Because of the timing, the firebug must have blocked the front first before entering the kitchen from the alley."

"If it was an inside job, it wasn't done by anyone who escaped with us," Rick concluded.

They heard the wail of an ambulance followed by the sirens of several police cruisers racing up Main Street. "Time for me to get to work," Preston said. "If any of you come up with a motive or a suspect, let me know. Right now, I've got to help secure the scene."

The big white rescue unit came up the street

from the opposite direction, just ahead of a second fire truck. Preston stepped out into the street and motioned to the approaching vehicles.

Less than a minute later the firemen were working to suppress the fire. Two EMTs, having gathered their equipment, approached Frank, then crouched next to him.

Rick stood back with Daniel. "Frank's probably our best witness and may have some of the answers. There's a chance he saw the arsonist before he got clocked."

"Preston will follow up," Daniel said, "but there's something I need to talk to you about. Is it possible that the man responsible for the scar on your face came back to try to finish the job?"

"No, he's dead," Rick said, "but some of the ones he worked for in the Mexican cartel avoided arrest. They're still at large and fighting for control of what's left of their criminal operation. You never really defeat that kind of evil."

"Any chance you were followed home?"

Rick expelled his breath in a slow hiss. "To the U.S., then all the way to Hartley? My gut says no. They know I can't work undercover anymore. I've been marked in a way that makes it impossible for me to hide my identity. More importantly, I'm no longer a threat to them, so there's no profit in taking me out. I doubt they'd waste their resources."

"All right then." Daniel glanced at the debris

strewed in every direction. "Taking on one of Hosteen Silver's boys is a bad idea, but taking *all* of us on is nothing short of a death wish. Whoever he is, he's going down."

"No doubt about it," Rick said. He looked over to where Kim stood watching the paramedics work. "I'm going to follow her to the hospital. I'd like to talk to her uncle as soon as he's conscious."

"Better wait for Preston. He's the only one of us who still carries a badge, and this is his turf, not ours," Daniel warned. "You know how he is about going by the book."

Rick gave his brother a mirthless smile. "Good for him. I started out that way, but undercover—"

"I know, but there are rules here," Daniel reminded him. "You're home now."

Daniel was right; he had to stand back. It wasn't his case.

Seeing Kim arguing with the paramedics, who wouldn't let her ride in the ambulance, he jogged over. "Come on, Kim, I'll take you to the hospital."

"Thanks, my car's at home."

As they strode to his rental SUV, Preston intercepted them. "Gene's going to take the women over to Level One Security, just in case it's a family threat. The kids will be brought over by the babysitters, too. Until we get a better handle on things, Daniel's office is like a fortress."

"What about Kim and the other two members of the tavern staff?" Rick asked.

"The servers have been told to stick around until I have the chance to ask them a few questions. Kim, you'll need to come back here after you check on your uncle's status," Preston said, looking directly at her. "Or you can meet me later tonight at the station. Your choice."

"I'll be sticking around at the hospital. If you need to speak to me before tomorrow, it'll have to be there."

"Fair enough. Under the circumstances, I don't blame you for wanting to stay close to your family, but it might be late before I make it to the hospital," Preston advised.

"As for you, Rick," Preston continued, "I'd like you to stick around. In your work I'm sure you've grown familiar with makeshift bombs, and I'd like you to go inside the building with me to help search for evidence."

Rick turned to Kim and held out his keys. "Take my SUV. It's the dark blue one toward the end of the block."

"Don't worry about it. I know Uncle Frank keeps a spare set of car keys. They're in a magnetic holder by the right front tire. It's okay if I take his car, isn't it?" she asked Preston.

"Yes. It'll have to be moved anyway once heavy

equipment is brought in to clear the rubble off the street," Preston answered.

"Good," Kim said. "I'll be at the hospital, probably all night, if anyone else needs me."

"I'll catch up to you later," Rick said, watching her hurry down the sidewalk to a parked car. Kim was great-looking, and had guts. He'd only just met her but he sure liked what he'd seen.

As Rick strode toward what was left of the building, he saw it was now illuminated by floodlights placed strategically along the street and inside the dining room. Going into agent mode, he stilled his thoughts and allowed a familiar coldness to envelop him.

He stopped by the front door and studied it without touching anything. "What kept this from opening?" he asked Preston, who'd jogged over to meet him after speaking to the Hartley Fire Department station chief.

"A pipe was wedged into the wrought-iron security grillwork on both sides of the door, barring it from the outside. I bagged and tagged it before anyone else besides Erin touched it. It'll need to be processed for prints."

"The chains on the outside kitchen doors…those being processed, too?" Rick asked.

"Yes, including the lock and the metal door hardware. It's all been tagged for the lab."

"All right, then, let's go into the kitchen. I only got a quick glance before we got out, so I'm still not sure what actually set off the explosion—an open flame, some kind of timer, or something else."

Preston led the way through the front entrance where a metal door dangled by the upper hinge. Broken chairs, table lamps, dishes, utensils and other items were scattered all around them.

As they started to pick their way across the interior, a tall man carrying a camera and wearing an H.F.D. jacket stepped out of the shadows.

"Stop. The kitchen area is off-limits to everyone except fire department personnel right now." He identified himself to Rick as the fire marshal. "There's no surveillance footage here, so it'll probably take me until tomorrow to compile my report on what caused the explosion. For now, you guys have to get out of here." Without another word, he strode into the kitchen.

"That's Arnie Medina," Preston said. "He has jurisdiction here at the scene, so let's leave the kitchen to him and we'll concentrate on evidence that might help us determine who the suspect was, or how long he was inside the building. That would give us a time line when tracking people who were in the area."

Rick glanced around at the wreckage. Over the past four years, deep undercover, he'd worked alongside people who would have slit his throat just for practice. He'd looked forward to coming home and no longer having to sleep with his weapon at arm's reach.

Now his much needed R&R would have to wait. His family was in the line of fire. The first attempt had failed, but experience taught him that killers seldom gave up until they succeeded—or were put down.

As they entered an employee area adjacent to the kitchen, Rick noticed a canvas tote next to the wall and lifted it out from behind a fallen roof tile. He looked inside and saw several textbooks. There was also a small purse along with a set of keys. He held up the purse so his brother could see. "Still dry. Somebody got lucky."

Preston took the wallet and located the driver's license. "It's Kim's. I hope she doesn't get stopped. I'll make sure to take it with me when I go to the hospital later tonight."

Rick nodded absently, then taking a closer look at the books, realized that one of the volumes was a textbook on police procedures, another on criminal law and a third one on evidence collection. "What's this all about?" he asked, surprised.

"Kim's working on an associate's degree in criminology. Her dad was one of ours, and she wants to follow in his footsteps. Jimmy Nelson was a good man."

"'Was'?"

"He was killed in the line of duty," Preston said, noticing a crime scene investigator waving him over. "I'll be back in a minute."

Rick hung the bag from a wall bracket that was still intact, minus a shelf, and continued to search. It was becoming increasingly difficult to stay alert this time of night. He'd spent most of the day on the road and was physically beat. He was running on pure adrenaline.

Preston motioned him outside. "I think you should consider staying with everyone else at Daniel's tonight. I've got a late night ahead of me."

"Do what you have to," Rick said. "I was thinking of stopping by the hospital and talking to Kim."

"No. Not until I question her." Preston took a breath and let it out slowly. "I won't bother telling you not to get involved in this case, Rick, because you already are, but you need to remember you're not FBI anymore. Most important of all, you have no concealed carry permit."

"Actually, I do. The Bureau made sure of that before I left."

"Okay, one less problem. Where's Kim's purse?"

"Inside," Rick answered, telling him the location.

"Okay," Preston said with a nod. "Considering this might yet track back to your past, let me know if you'll feel safer carrying a badge just in case you have to mix it up with someone. I'm pretty sure the chief would deputize you, considering you're a highly trained former special agent with a distinguished record."

"Good. Do that as soon as you can. It'll be good backup."

"Consider it done. So, will you be going to Daniel's?" Preston asked.

He shook his head. "If someone's after me..." He let the sentence hang.

"There's no safer place on this earth than Daniel's compound," Preston told him, as if the issue was settled. He looked toward the brother in question, who was coming up the sidewalk.

For the first time since the blast, Rick smiled. Out of all his Navajo foster brothers, Daniel, the owner of a major security company, was the one he understood best. "I hear your place is as secure as Fort Knox."

"Did you expect anything less?" Daniel said as he stopped in front of them. "Speaking of safety, Rick, you're driving a rental SUV, but considering what happened tonight, you'd be better off with something from my company's motor pool. Tomorrow I'll match you up with a more suitable ride."

Preston excused himself and went to interview the two waiting employees, while Daniel walked with Rick back to the rental.

"Death follows me," Rick said as he climbed

into the SUV. "Undercover, that's a given, but I never expected to find it here." His lips straightened into a thin hard line. "I guess they don't realize it yet."

"What?"

"Hosteen Silver's boys are damned hard to kill."

Chapter Two

After spending a restless night, Rick headed to the kitchen for coffee, desperate for a shot of caffeine.

Paul and Preston's adopted sons, Jason and Bobby, were playing a loud video game in the next room, and as he poured himself a mug of the dark steamy brew, Daniel intercepted him.

"Come on, time to work. This way."

Rick followed his brother into the main room, the office's planning and computer center. A huge horizontal computer screen the size of a table rested adjacent to four large monitors on the wall.

"I have access to intelligence chatter, courtesy of my Department of Homeland Security and National Security Agency contacts. There's been nothing at all to indicate you were specifically targeted last night. I contacted the Bureau, as well, and their sources agree with the other agencies. No flags were raised," Daniel said.

"So they might have been hoping to kill everyone, or maybe only one or two of us, while the rest of the family became collateral damage," Rick said. "That's pretty cold."

"There's no way to be certain, but my instincts are telling me that if they wanted one of us specifically, they would have taken their shot before now," Daniel said. "Their real target could have also been Frank, Kim, one of the two servers or the Brickhouse Tavern itself."

"The timing was linked to my homecoming, though," Rick said. "Besides that, was there anything special about last night?"

"Not that we know of," Daniel said, "but if your theory is right and this has nothing to do with your undercover work, then we should be looking for an enemy you made here, maybe during one of your infrequent visits."

"I can't think of anyone," Rick said, shaking his head, "but I'll give it some thought."

Preston came in just then. "Frank Nelson still can't be questioned. He's out of danger, according to the doctors, but they want to keep him sedated and are monitoring him closely for swelling of the brain. Kim gave us a preliminary statement late last night, but she was too shaken to remember anything we don't already know."

"It was close to home for her, but if she's going to be a cop, she'll have to toughen up fast," Rick said, his voice heavy.

Preston looked at his brother. "She will, but she's

barely out of the starting gate. Her dad's gone and right now her uncle's her only living relative. The incident last night turned her world upside down."

For a moment Rick found himself indulging in an emotion he seldom experienced—sympathy. He knew what it was like to suddenly find yourself all alone.

"I'd still like to talk to her. Kim may know something useful. I'm not a cop, at least not anymore, so that might set her at ease and help her remember some details," Rick said.

Preston nodded. "Go for it."

"Before anyone leaves, we need to decide if our families need extra protection," Daniel said.

"I spoke to Gene this morning, and he agrees with me," Preston said. "The best solution is to get them out of town. Fortunately, Kendra has her U.S. Marshals training, so she'll keep them safe," Preston added, referring to Paul's wife. "We can also send two of your top security people along with them, Daniel, just to make sure."

"Where are you planning to send them?" Rick asked.

"To Gene's ranch," Preston replied. "You've never been there, Rick, but it's in Colorado, a few hours from here, out in open country where intruders are easily spotted."

"Since the trouble his wife, Lori, had a few years back, Gene's place now has surveillance cameras that feed to our computers here," Daniel explained. "With some handpicked men, and Gene and Kendra on the job, they'll be safe."

"Good plan," Rick said.

Paul came in just then. He still favored his shoulder when he moved, the result of the gunshot that had forced him to retire from the U.S. Marshals Service. "I'll be monitoring things from here."

"I'll handle the details," Daniel said, then looked at Rick. "You're going to need one of our special SUVs. Just leave the rental here and one of my men will take care of it. I've got a black one outside that'll be perfect for you. It's got extra Kevlar armor, a GPS tracker and run-flat tires."

"Good. I'd like to get going," Rick admitted.

"They wouldn't let Kim in to be with her uncle after I spoke with her last night, so she went home," Preston said. "If Kim isn't at the hospital this morning, you'll find her at Silver Heritage Jewelry and Gifts. The shop is owned by a member of our tribe, a Navajo woman, Angelina Curley."

"So Kim has two jobs, one at the Brickhouse and one at a jewelry store?" he asked.

"She's paying her way through college with gigs that let her keep flexible hours," Preston answered.

"I know she thinks highly of you. What's the story there?" Rick asked Preston.

"I put the man who shot her dad behind bars. Her uncle Frank really stepped up for her after that, but the P.D. kept an eye on her, as well. We wanted Kim to know that officers take care of our own, and if she needed anything, she had help. After she enlisted in the army out of high school, we kept in touch. She was deployed for a few years and then came home determined to follow in her dad's footsteps."

"So I should treat her with kid gloves, is that it?" Rick asked. It was a fair question, and there was no rancor in his voice.

"No, not at all. Just be aware that she's got a lot of officers watching out for her."

Daniel tossed Rick a set of keys. "Check in when you can. As soon as I get the family squared away, I'm going to dig into the backgrounds of each of the players, including Kim and her uncle. I have the contacts and clearance to get into databases the PD can't access without a truckload of paperwork."

Rick walked out and found the black SUV. It had a lot of extras and must have cost his brother's company a lot of money, but he was glad to have it. Something was telling him the case would be getting even messier soon.

As he drove down Hartley's Main Street, one thought continued to nag at him. He had to know if he'd somehow been responsible—if his arrival in Hartley had set off the attack. Maybe his instincts were still on overdrive, but he'd learned not to ignore them. They'd kept him alive.

KIM WAS CLEANING the glass-topped display case when she heard the bell over the door jingle. Glancing up, she saw Rick stride in and nod to Fred, the security guard, who was standing nearby.

She smiled. Rick had that elusive "it" quality that commanded attention without even trying. He'd been her secret crush back in high school. Rick had been the larger-than-life high school quarterback, and she'd been the nerdy freshman buried in homework. Back then, between her thick glasses and her braces, she'd barely got a glance from the popular guys. Of course, it also could have been because her father was a cop.

The boy she'd watched from a distance was gone now, and in his place stood a sexy, earthy, dangerous-looking man. The scar made him look tough, seasoned by a hard life and infinitely masculine.

As he walked around the counter in her direction, she couldn't take her eyes off him. He moved without wasted motion, sure of himself, aware of his surroundings.

When he saw her he smiled and for a moment his face gentled, but the emotion was gone in a flash.

"Good morning, Rick. What can I do for you?" she asked, going up to him.

"I know the police have already interviewed you, Kim, but I'd like to discuss last night again.

When do you take your next break?" he asked in a voice so low only she could hear.

She glanced at the clock. Angelina wasn't in yet, so it wouldn't hurt to take her fifteen minutes a little early, particularly since they had no customers at the moment.

"Now would be fine."

She went to the coffeepot in the corner and offered him a cup. When he shook his head, she poured herself one. "I've been thinking of nothing else but the explosion. I barely slept last night, but I still haven't been able to remember anything that might help the police."

"Then shift your focus. Don't think about the explosion. Concentrate on what happened earlier that evening."

"Okay." As she looked into his eyes she saw something there that made her hold her breath. The angry scar across his face spoke of life-and-death struggles, but his steady gaze shone with strength, courage and determination.

"Your brother Preston asked the hospital staff for permission to speak to Uncle Frank last night, but the doctors refused. They had to sedate him. He was so scared, waking up in the emergency room."

"Did you get to talk to him at all?"

"For a bit. Uncle Frank told me he caught a glimpse of a big man wearing overalls, a blue ball cap and mirrored sunglasses right before he was hit on the back of the head. I should have asked him more, but all I could think of was how lucky we were. We'd all nearly died." She stopped and looked up at him. "Does that make me sound like a coward?"

"It makes you sound human. When it counted, you stepped up. Your first thought was to find your uncle, then you did everything you could to get him out of danger. You worked to save a life, and did a lot more than was expected of you. In my book, that's the definition of a hero."

She shook her head and gave him a quick half smile. "Thanks, but no. There were no heroes there. We were all just people doing what we had to do."

"It was a crazy time," he said quietly.

"The person who did this took a huge risk. If my uncle hadn't had the Cowboys game going full blast, he probably would have heard the guy sneak up behind him."

Hearing the jingle at the front door, they both glanced in that direction and saw the security guard hold the door open for Angelina. "That's my boss," she said quietly. "She's got a bad temper, so I better get back to work. We can meet later for lunch at the Desert Rose Café and talk some more if you want."

Rick looked at Angelina and suddenly remembered meeting her before. Smiling, he went up to her. "Angelina Tso! I'm not sure if you remember me," he said. "You got stuck in Copper Canyon after a hard rain several years ago after working with my father, and I towed you out to the highway."

"I'm Angelina Curley now," she said curtly.

"Weren't you studying with Hosteen Silver to become a medicine woman?" Rick asked, using the Navajo equivalent of Mister that most of their tribe preferred. "Did you find another mentor after my foster father's death?"

Her expression darkened, and Kim, who'd been watching the exchange, recognized the signs instantly.

"Kim, I'm paying you to work, so find something to do!" Angelina snapped. "And you," she added, looking at Rick. "I'm warning you right now to stay out of my store. Neither you nor your family is welcome here. Hosteen Silver cheated me. He took my money and then wouldn't let me come back for more instruction. He robbed me of my chance to become a Navajo healer, then tried to ruin my reputation."

"There's got to be more to the story. *Integrity* was more than a word to Hosteen Silver," he said, biting back his anger. "Why don't we talk about this in private?"

"I'm not saying another word to you. Fred, show Mr. Cloud out," Angelina said, looking at the security guard.

"I know my foster father, and what you're telling me isn't something he'd do. Let's talk and figure things out," Rick insisted, taking a step closer to her and gesturing to the empty office behind them. "We can talk in private in there."

"Keep your hands off me," Angelina shouted at him.

"He didn't—" Kim started, but in an instant everything went crazy.

As Fred rushed forward, squaring off in front of Rick, fists clenched, Kim squeezed in between them, facing the security guard.

"Fred, he didn't touch her. Just calm down," Kim urged, anxious to avoid a stupid confrontation.

"Do something, you fool," Angelina yelled at Fred.

"Out of my way, Kim," the security guard ordered.

"No. Just chill out, Fred, okay?"

"Throw him out, damn you!" Angelina screamed.

The guard grabbed Kim by the shoulders and pushed her aside. Kim stumbled and slammed her ribs against the edge of the counter. Groaning, she reached out with both hands and, getting a grip on the display case, managed not to fall.

Rick instantly grabbed the man by the belt and collar and hurled him facedown across the tiled floor.

Fred careened into a freestanding metal display filled with souvenirs and cheap Mexican pottery. The display rocked, sending a cascade of key chains, postcards and clay pots tumbling to the floor.

Angelina reached for the low shelf behind the front counter, brought out a revolver and pointed it directly at Rick. She was breathing hard, shaking and clearly out of control.

"No!" Kim lunged toward her boss, but Rick beat her to it.

In a blur he yanked the weapon from Angelina's hand and looked over at the guard, who'd grabbed the display and managed to keep it from tipping over.

"Everyone, *calm down!*" he ordered, opening the cylinder and dumping the bullets onto the floor before placing the revolver on the counter.

Kim froze in place. Even without a weapon, he still commanded the room. "I'm leaving now," he said, holding out his hand, palm up, as a signal for Fred to stay put. "See you at lunch, Miss Nelson?" he asked softly. Assessing the situation with a steely gaze, he never turned his back until he was out of the shop.

As the door swung shut, Angelina, still shaking,

turned to Fred, who was down on one knee picking up the scattered merchandise. "You're my brother's son so I gave you a chance, but you stink as a security guard. Turn in your gear and get out. You're fired." Then she turned to Kim. "And you—"

"Angelina, I didn't do anything wrong this morning, and you know it." She wasn't going to take any abuse from the woman, but she couldn't afford to lose her job. If she could only manage to calm her down....

"He came to see *you*."

"All he wanted to do was follow up on last night," Kim said, struggling to keep her voice low and controlled. "That explosion at the Brickhouse could have killed fifteen people. Most of us got lucky, but my uncle is in the hospital with a fractured skull. You must have seen the burned-out building and street barricades. We were lucky to get out alive."

"You were hosting a dinner for the sons of Hosteen Silver. What did you expect? That bunch brings nothing but bad luck. Look what just happened here," Angelina said, then shook her head. "Forget it. Get out. You're fired."

"I doubt Mr. Cloud will ever be coming back, so why let me go?" she insisted. If she ended up jobless, how would she be able to stay in school?

"I'm not interested in an employee who's friends with my enemies. I know you're having lunch with him," she snapped. "I'll mail your last paycheck. Now get out."

Kim picked up her purse, jacket and lunch bag and walked out while Angelina searched for the bullets still scattered on the floor.

"I'M GLAD YOU called to tell me what happened, Rick," Preston said, looking around the interior of the Desert Rose Café, studying the smattering of diners there.

"I had to. That woman lost it completely. When she screamed at me to take my hands off her, her guard moved in, but I never touched Angelina Curley. Kim can verify what happened," Rick said, reaching for his spicy breakfast burrito.

"Angelina's well known around town and has friends in high places despite her erratic behavior. Stay away from her. It's unlikely that she's involved in what happened at the Brickhouse, so tread carefully. You don't want to turn her into an enemy."

"We already are enemies." His gaze snapped to the shop across the street as an old saying played in his mind. "Hell hath no fury like a woman scorned." One way or another, he was going to find out what had happened between Angelina and Hosteen Silver.

Chapter Three

Though it was only ten-thirty and way too early for lunch, with nowhere else to go at the moment, Kim decided to stop by the Desert Rose Café for a cup of tea. As she walked in, she was surprised to see Preston and Rick sitting at a table near the window.

Kim approached them slowly, wondering if she was making a mistake. Maybe Rick was bad luck. Look at everything that had happened so far, and he'd only been in town since yesterday afternoon.

She discarded the thought immediately. There was no such thing as luck. She remembered the quote by Louis Pasteur her father had hung in his office at home. "Chance favors the prepared mind." People made their own luck.

Rick and Preston stood as she came over, and Rick gestured to the chair beside him. "What brings you by so early, Kim? If you're hungry, I can recommend the breakfast burrito. It's terrific. The coffee…not so much."

She smiled. "I know. I usually order tea."

The waitress came over and smiled. "Hey, Kim. What'll you have?"

"How about a job, Sally? Only kidding. I just got fired," she said, "so a cup of honey tea will do."

"I'm so sorry to hear that," the young waitress answered.

"So am I," Rick added. "Order what you want and consider it part of my apology. I owe you that, at least."

Kim shook her head. "Tea will be enough." As the waitress left, she touched Rick's arm briefly. "I appreciate the offer, but all you really did was speed up the inevitable. I've never liked the way Angelina treated her employees and, frankly, I only stuck around because the work fit my schedule."

Preston spoke up. "If you need some financial help—"

She shook her head and held up a hand, interrupting him. "I've got skills and experience working retail, so I'll find a new job soon. However, if you hear of a part-time position with flexible hours, let me know."

"I've got to get back to work," Preston said, removing a few dollars from his wallet and placing them on the table. "Kim, keep thinking hard about last night. Sometimes the answers don't come all at once."

"I will."

As the waitress brought over her cup of tea, Kim eyed the piece of Rick's burrito that remained but said nothing. Pride always stopped her from asking for favors or help.

"We changed our minds. How about a breakfast burrito for the lady, too," he said.

"Be back in a jiff," the waitress said.

Kim smiled at Rick. "You didn't have to do that, but thanks. The aromas in here always make me hungry."

"No problem. Now I feel a little less guilty."

A lengthy silence ensued until Sally returned with her food and, wanting to know more about Rick, Kim decided to start the conversation. "So tell me, Rick. Are you really home for good?" she asked, taking a bite of burrito.

"Yes."

"Are you glad to be back among family or do you miss your old job?"

"Both."

He obviously wasn't much for small talk. She took several more bites, enjoying the flavorful explosion of green chili. Remembering how procedural books said that people often opened up just to fill the lapse in conversation, she let the silence stretch.

It didn't work. Rick had probably read the same book years ago.

"I appreciate that you bought me something to eat and are letting me enjoy the burrito in peace, but I get the feeling there's something on your mind," she said, taking the last bite. "So how can I help you?"

"I know Angelina Curley had dealings with my foster father, then one day she stopped coming around," he said. "I don't believe her accusations at all. Any idea what really happened between them?"

"I've heard pieces of the story here and there, but because they originated from Angelina I'm not sure how accurate they are," she warned.

"Go on."

"Hosteen Silver accepted cash and jewelry in payment for her instruction and apprenticeship, but then, according to Angelina, he made sexual advances. When she rejected him, he got angry and refused to continue her training."

"My foster father would never have done anything like that. The woman's lying."

"Uncle Frank knew your foster father. I met him once at the Brickhouse, too. He didn't strike me as that type of person, either," she admitted. "But in my experience, Angelina isn't above lying if it suits her. I've seen how she twists things around when she's dealing with customers and vendors. She keeps things legal, but she's completely unethical," Kim said. "Maybe she was the one who made a pass and got shot down. She doesn't take rejection well, I can tell you that. Or maybe she just didn't have what it takes to be a medicine woman and needed someone to blame. Considering Angelina doesn't remember details, I'm surprised she's as successful in business as she is. She'll often ask us the same question two or three times."

"That might explain her failure as my father's apprentice. The Sings have to be memorized perfectly and some last for days," Rick answered. "One mistake and the gods won't answer, or they might make things worse for a person out of anger. Getting it right shows respect."

"It took days for her to remember the combination of the new safe." She paused for a moment. "Angelina's not stupid, far from it, but she's easily distracted."

"My foster father could be very exacting. If Angelina wasn't measuring up, he would have told her that in no uncertain terms."

"Angelina would have blamed him, not herself," she answered.

"I was surprised to see her pull a gun this morning. Was that all a bluff, or is she capable of violence?" he asked.

"I don't think she would have fired at you. She's a bully and wanted you afraid. If you'd started pleading with her to set it down, that would have made her feel in control, and you would have made her day."

"I get it."

"For what it's worth, that's my amateur attempt at profiling. Although I've worked at Silver Heritage for the past ten months, she and I aren't friends, or even friendly. I don't even recall having a conversation with her that wasn't business-related."

"Fair enough," Rick said.

Kim watched him for a moment. He knew a lot about her, but she'd yet to learn much about him. Mystery clung to Rick like dust from a hot summer's whirlwind.

"I think my brother said something about Angelina owning another business as well as Silver Heritage," he said.

"That's true. She has a high-end Southwest design jewelry business across from the regional hospital. If you want, we can go over there after I finish class. The manager's a friend of mine. Although Angelina goes over there every day just after lunch, she usually comes back to the downtown shop after an hour or so. If you let me come along, I can watch out for her."

She checked her watch. "Right now I've got to walk over to campus. I've got class at noon."

"Mind if I tag along? It's a nice day to be outside."

"Glad for the company."

After they left the café, he fell into step beside

her. It was a beautiful October day and the air was brisk but not cold. "So tell me, what makes you so determined to become a cop?"

"I want a career doing work that matters."

He nodded. "And you think you can make a difference as a cop."

It hadn't been a question, but she answered him anyway. "Good people are needed to keep the bad ones in check."

He smiled. "That's what Hosteen Silver used to say. It's part of the Navajo belief that says balance is necessary for happiness."

Rick's entire face softened when he smiled. The edginess that was so much a part of him disappeared and gave place to calmness. It even made his scar look less daunting. "You should smile more often, Rick."

He grew serious again. "I don't usually have many reasons to do that."

"Then find them," she answered with a smile of her own.

Seeing a homeless man she recognized sitting on the sidewalk against the wall of a laundry, soaking up the sunshine, she quickened her pace. "That's Mike. I brought him leftover food every night at the end of my shift at the Brickhouse. He's going to have to find other help now."

As they neared, the man looked over then

jumped to his feet. "Mike, don't go. I need to talk to you," she called out.

The homeless man stood around six feet tall, with a red beard and brown hair. He was wearing a camouflage jacket, jeans, lace-up boots and was carrying a backpack.

Mike glanced at her, then Rick. A second later he stepped off the sidewalk into the alley and disappeared.

As they reached the alley, they saw his back just for an instant before he slipped around the far corner of the building.

"Rats!" she grumbled. "The weather's going to be turning cold pretty soon. Mike's going to need food and shelter. We have a food pantry over on 4th Street that feeds the homeless, but they already have to turn people away. One of the churches plans to take up the slack, though, and I wanted to make sure he knew."

"Mike is behind the Brickhouse every night?" Rick asked quickly.

"Yeah. He always sits on the steps of the furniture store's loading dock, waiting for me to come out into the alley."

"If he was there last night, he may have seen something important," Rick said. "Maybe even the guy who clobbered Frank and sabotaged the gas line. We have to find him again."

"That's going to be tough. You saw how he can

disappear in a flash," she said. "I know I mentioned talking to him, but except for a few rare times, it was mostly a one-way conversation. My guess is that even if he saw something, he won't talk about it."

"He may be emotionally disturbed. Whatever the situation, I want to talk to him," Rick said. "Even if all he does is nod or shake his head, it might be enough to give us a lead."

"Good luck."

SEVERAL MINUTES LATER they arrived at the small community college campus and walked up the wide sidewalk toward a large, white, concrete-and-stone building. "This is my stop." Kim met his gaze. "If you find Mike, be kind but careful around him. Some things can't be forced. He's been living on the street for years now, and he's wary of everyone."

"It never hurts to try. Did you ever learn his last name?"

"I don't even know what his real first name is. I've always admired the football player Michael Oher, particularly after seeing *The Blind Side,* so I asked him if I could call him Mike. He nodded."

"All right. Let's see what I can do."

She checked her watch. "I've got to go. Class lasts an hour. Should we meet afterward and go to Turquoise Dreams, Angelina's other shop?"

"Okay, sounds good."

"See you later, then," she said.

AFTER LEAVING CAMPUS, Rick headed back to the center of town, deliberately choosing the side streets and alleys along Main, watching carefully as he approached restaurants and fast-food establishments. Mike undoubtedly already knew about the explosion at the Brickhouse Tavern and would be searching for a new place to score a meal.

At first Rick had no luck, but eventually he spotted Mike standing on a wooden pallet as he searched through the big green trash bin behind Hamburger Haven.

Instead of approaching him, Rick circled the block and came up the alley, looking down at the pavement and never making eye contact. About twenty feet away, he sat on a flattened cardboard box, his back to the wall. He was wearing a turtlenecked sweater and jeans, not his usual jacket, which often served to hide a handgun at his waist. Instead he had it in his boot for emergencies, but he knew what he was dealing with here and doubted there'd be a problem. Unless cornered, with no escape possible, Mike was unlikely to turn violent. He'd run. Though Rick pretended to be looking toward the street, he could see Mike in his peripheral vision. He knew that Mike, aware of him from the moment he'd entered the alley, had been watching him.

As Mike stepped down off the pallet, Rick saw the tattoo on the man's left forearm. It was the outline of a horse head with a diagonal line beneath it—the insignia of the Army's First Cavalry division.

"Ooorah, soldier," Rick said in a barely audible voice.

Mike looked at him, his gaze focusing on Rick's scar.

"Some scars are easier to see than others," Rick said, still avoiding direct eye contact. "You like cheeseburgers? I'm hungry. I'm going to get myself one. I'll pick one up for you, too, if you want."

Rick glanced at Mike and noted the vacant expression on his face. For a moment he wondered if the man was beyond the ability to answer questions.

Then it happened. A spark of intelligence lit up Mike's face for an instant. Rick realized that what he'd seen before was the thousand-yard stare: the blank look of someone who'd seen too much suffering and death.

"Cheeseburger. And fries," Mike said.

"Coming right up."

Rick went inside the small fast-food place, eager to return but afraid to look as though he was in a hurry. He'd just found his first asset and, with luck, he'd also be able to help the man.

One thing he knew about was adversity. It either broke or remade you, but sometimes finding your strength again required retreating to a place so deep inside yourself, the world couldn't reach you. He understood that. He'd done it himself.

When Rick returned to the alley, Mike was gone, but Rick could sense he was being watched. Mike was nearby, probably trying to make up his mind about him. Rick placed the sandwich bag filled with food on a cardboard box next to the wall where he'd been sitting. Mike would find it there.

"I'm after the man who nearly killed Kim, her uncle and my family," Rick called out as clearly as possible without shouting. "You see things most of us miss, Mike. Whatever you tell me will stay between us, but I could really use your help. Whoever it is may not be through yet."

Rick left the alley and crossed the street. As an undercover operative he'd lived engulfed by a darkness most sane people would do anything to avoid. Yet it was there, in that world of senseless violence, that the true measure of a man was often found…and sometimes lost.

Chapter Four

Rick picked up a soft drink inside the fast food place, then walked back to where he'd left Daniel's loaner SUV. He'd drive rather than walk back to campus. With time to spare, he took the long way, reacquainting himself with Hartley. Eventually he pulled into campus.

When he'd taken classes here right out of high school, the community college had been nothing more than a multi-classroom structure and administration building. Now the campus comprised about three acres, with a grassy commons area and central fountain.

Rick took the road leading to the visitors' parking area and pulled into the first slot he found. After a short walk, he found Kim standing just down the hall talking to a man who looked vaguely familiar. It hit him a moment later when the guy turned and Rick saw his face clearly for the first time.

"Karl Edmonds. It's been a lifetime," Rick said.

"You know my professor?" Kim asked.

"*Professor?* That's one career I never would have expected you to choose," Rick said, looking at Karl.

"I'm technically an instructor, Cloud. I teach part-time, and work full-time for the Hartley P.D. I run the bomb squad," he said.

"Now *that* fits the kid I knew," Rick said.

Karl looked at the scar that ran across Rick's face, then glanced away quickly. "Looks like you came in second in a knife fight, dude. Hope you've brushed up on your hand-to-hand since then."

Rick remembered why Karl had always annoyed him. They'd always been competitors, never really friends. Karl's biggest problem, which had obviously followed him into manhood, was that he never knew when to shut up.

"We'd better get going. Kim and I need to meet with Preston," Rick said.

"It was good seeing you, buddy," Karl said.

"I'm sure we'll run into each other again." Rick held Karl's gaze for a moment longer than necessary. Instinct was telling him to be careful around the man. Was it that old competition between them or something more? He couldn't tell, but until he figured it out, he wouldn't lower his guard.

KIM FOLLOWED HIM to his SUV. "You and Karl… You weren't ever really friends, were you?"

"No, but we attended school together and played on the same football team. We were friendly—at times."

"I can't believe how rude he was to you," Kim said. "Do you really need to meet your brother or was that an excuse to walk away?"

"Both. It's a bad idea to make enemies with someone Preston may have to depend on someday," he said. "Right now, I'd also like to get clearance to take a look around the Brickhouse again in daylight," he said. "Afterward we'll head to Turquoise Dreams. Angelina certainly got my attention today."

"Are you sure your brother's going to be okay with you investigating on your own?"

"Under ordinary circumstances, no, but the Hartley P.D. is badly understaffed. I can be an asset to them because I've got the best law-enforcement training in the world."

"Will I need clearance, too?"

"Yes. I need you there because you're familiar with the place and can help me reconstruct the scene. If something's off or doesn't belong there, it might stick out to you but slip right past me."

As THEY RODE to the station, she remained quiet. Although she never looked directly at him, Kim was aware of the way his strong hands gripped the wheel and how he seemed to completely focus on whatever he was doing at the time. She wondered what he would be like in bed—all that intensity, all that drive.... Everything about him spoke of endurance and masculinity.

She shifted in her seat. This was not the time for thoughts such as these. Still watching him out of the corner of her eye, she saw him rub the bottom tip of the scar near his cheek.

"Does it ever ache?"

"What?" he asked, focusing on her.

"The scar."

"Not generally. The skin around it feels tight sometimes, but that's about it." He glanced at her, then back at the road. "When we first met, you never looked directly at it. Most people stare when they see me for the first time, then try to pretend they weren't."

"Your eyes drew me more," she said.

"My...what?"

"You have a way of looking through people, not at them."

"I observe. It's how I stay alive."

"Is the scar one of the reasons you left the Bureau?"

"Yeah, it ruined me for undercover work. I became too easily identifiable."

"You could have still been involved in routine investigative work," she said. "Why leave?"

"I preferred undercover assignments." He shook

his head. "No, it was more than that. I knew it was time for me to come home and try to reconnect."

"With your brothers?"

"With myself."

THEY ARRIVED AT the police station a short while later and Rick led her down the hall to his brother's office. Preston waved them inside.

"Anything new?" Rick asked.

"No, but it's too soon. The lab's backlogged."

"I'd like clearance to search the crime scene," Rick said. "I know the arson investigator and your crime scene team has already been through there, but maybe Kim and I will see something that'll trigger a memory. It can't hurt."

"You're right. In fact, I've already asked my captain about getting you officially involved. He's agreed."

Preston reached into the drawer and brought out a shield. "I'm deputizing you. Raise your right hand." Preston swore him in with a short phrase.

"At the end of this case, if you want to join the force officially, your application will go to the top of the pile."

"Thanks."

Preston looked over at Kim. "Stay with Rick and follow his orders to the letter. You are *not* a police officer, you're just an observer."

"Understood," she said.

"All right." Preston looked at his brother. "Remember to wear gloves," he added, handing him and Kim a pair each.

After they left the station, Rick asked, "What were the names of the servers last night?"

"Bobby Crawford and Kate Masters."

"How do we find them?"

"Kate's probably in class right now. She carries a heavier load than I do and is just a few credit hours away from her business degree. She probably won't be much help. Kate's a hard worker, but her mind's always on some test or paper. She rarely even goes into the kitchen."

"What about Crawford?"

"Bobby comes in on time and does his job, but never has much to say. We don't talk about anything other than job-related things."

As they neared what remained of the Brickhouse, Rick slowed down to study the heavily damaged structure before parking across the street.

"Look down the alley. The back wall was pretty much blown out last night, but it looks even worse this morning. More bricks and roof beams must have come down since then. The loading dock and half the alley are blocked."

"At least all that flying debris didn't penetrate the side wall of the furniture store. These old downtown buildings were built to last," Kim noted.

"Well, whoever cut the gas line and blocked the

door counted on the initial blast and resulting fire to do their work," he said. "If we hadn't escaped and lived to tell the real story, it might have been written off as an accident caused by faulty connections."

Kim peered ahead at a young man ducking beneath the tape and walking into the alley. "I think that's Bobby Crawford. See him over there? He's wearing jeans, a gray sweatshirt and ball cap," she said, pointing.

Rick caught a glimpse of the man just as he climbed over a pile of rubble and headed toward the loading dock. "Come on. Let's go talk to him."

By the time they'd crossed the street and reached the crime scene barrier, Bobby was nowhere in sight. Rick slipped beneath the crime scene tape and climbed up the rubble-filled stairs of the loading dock to look inside.

"Stay here," Rick said, then slipped though the gaping hole where the blown-out kitchen doors had once stood.

Rick moved slowly and carefully, picking his way through the mess. Only a few wall studs and pieces of wallboard remained between the kitchen and the dining room. The left wall of the kitchen facing the street had also lost most of its roof structure. From where he stood, Rick could see blue sky and part of the parapet. As he turned to look back out into the alley, Rick noticed that the remaining outside brick wall on both sides of the gap was bowed, ready to crumble.

At the far end of the dining area was a set of brick-littered stairs leading down into the basement. Except for a few inches of water, it was probably the least damaged room in the tavern.

He stood still for a moment, listening. Someone was going through the rubble in the north end of the dining area, the side farthest from the street and hidden by the remaining walls. He turned toward the sound. Despite his size, Rick could move silently when he hunted man or beast. He had a tattoo over his heart with the word *chaha'oh*. It meant shadow.

"Federal agent. Don't move." As he stepped through what remained of the doorway, he realized he'd spoken out of habit. He was now working with the Hartley Police. "Turn around slowly."

"Just don't shoot, okay? I work here," he said. "Remember me from last night? I'm Bobby. Bobby Crawford."

Hearing footsteps behind him, Rick turned his head for a second and saw Kim. She'd come in the same way he had, through the door cavity, and was wearing a white hard hat and holding another.

"Dude, just chill, okay?" Bobby said, his hands up. "In the rush to get out last night, I lost something important. I was hoping to find it before they brought in the bulldozers. It was a gift from my mom."

Rick sized Bobby up in a glance. He was around eighteen or nineteen, stood five foot six and had dark hair and brown eyes.

"Did you mention this to the police when they took your statement?"

"No, I didn't realize it was gone until this morning. It's a gold crucifix I wear around my neck on a chain."

"You shouldn't be here. That's why the yellow tape's there," Rick snapped. "It's not safe for the public to be rummaging around, moving things around."

"Dude, are you *listening?* It's not evidence. It's a family heirloom."

"Forensic experts and the fire marshal will continue to sort through the debris and recover items. If your crucifix is found, you'll get it back," Rick told him. "Let me see your driver's license."

When Bobby handed it over, Rick took a quick look, then returned it. "All right. Get going. If anything belonging to you turns up, I know how to find you."

Bobby backed out through the kitchen and quickly disappeared down the steps.

"I ran into the fire marshal out on the sidewalk," Kim said, and handed Rick the hard hat. "Preston had called to tell him we'd be here, so Medina came over to make sure we followed safety protocols. He said no one's allowed inside the Brickhouse without hard hats and he intends to stand by until we're ready to leave."

Rick gave her a tight-lipped smile. "Medina give you hard time?"

"No, not really," she replied softly, gesturing to the street to indicate the man was close by. "He told me not to lean on anything or to move any structural elements. Then he gave me these and insisted we wear them."

"All right," he said, putting the hard hat on. "Let's take a look around, then we'll go into the kitchen, where all this started."

She stood in one spot and turned around in a circle, slowly surveying the wreckage. "I can't believe what this place has become. You could always hear laughter here."

"Everyone's okay and we have another chance at life. That's a reason for laughter. You ready to go into the kitchen?"

She nodded. They picked their way back, stepping over and around the remnants of the shattered interior.

They were barely in the kitchen when Arnie Medina poked his head in through the front door and yelled. "This place is coming down! Get out. *Now!*"

Rick grabbed Kim's hand and moved toward

the gap in the wall facing the alley. Before they could reach the opening, a cloud of dust descended and bricks began to tumble from overhead, raining down on their escape route.

Rick turned back toward the dining area when a roof beam sagged, then cracked as the ceiling gave way.

Chapter Five

Rick spun Kim around and pushed her toward the basement stairs. "Down! Jump!"

Because the wooden steps were littered with chunks of bricks and debris, Rick and Kim ended up sliding into the basement, flat on their backs. As dust and ash billowed down the steps with them, Rick rolled on top of Kim, his body protecting her from the building materials that bounced down the steps. One brick struck his hard hat like a stone fist.

Within seconds the earthshaking cascade was replaced by a loud rattle, then a dozen or more solid thumps from somewhere above. When it was quiet again, Rick rose and looked down at Kim, who still had her eyes tightly shut. It was a good thing, considering her face was covered with dust.

"Keep your eyes shut and I'll blow away some of the dust."

He tried, but they both started coughing. He helped her sit up.

For a moment she kept her head down. Finally she opened her eyes and looked up at him. "We're alive, I take it?"

Rick smiled. "Pretty much. You okay?"

"I feel like I just went down a rock slide, but all I've got are bumps and bruises, I guess," she said, looking down at herself.

Shaken, she turned to look at the stairs. They were piled high with bricks and rubble, but light was coming in as the dust began to disperse.

"At least we're not totally trapped," Rick commented. "But we're going to need help digging out of here."

"Can you hear me?" came a man's voice from up above.

"I hear you, Medina, and we're both fine. There's a lot of debris in the way, but once we clear a path we'll have enough room to crawl out," Rick called back.

"No! Don't start moving things around. Something else could come down. Wait until my people have a chance to check the situation up here. Stay away from the stairs, hang tight and we'll get you out."

TWENTY-FIVE MINUTES later Rick and Kim were standing in the alley at the rear of the Brickhouse. The firemen had braced the remaining walls as well as the sagging roof beams, then cleared a path for them.

"Did I ever tell you how much I *hate* closed-in spaces? I felt like I was smothering down there," she said, coughing.

"That was poor air quality, not claustrophobia," he said, clearing his throat. "At least you did all the right things, including the most important of all—keeping your head."

Arnie Medina came to meet them. "Speaking of keeping your heads, good thing I handed you the hard hats, huh?"

"Yeah, but I still don't get it. I made sure we stayed in sections that looked stable," Rick said.

"You had someone working against you. A guy with mirrored sunglasses, dressed in sweatpants and a gray sweatshirt, gave it a push with a two-by-six. He stopped the second I saw him and yelled, but I have no idea how long he was out there."

"Wait. Sweatpants or jeans?" Rick asked, instantly thinking of Bobby.

"No way," Kim said, reading Rick's thoughts.

"You know who it was?" Medina asked.

"Maybe," Rick answered. "What color hair? Height? Give me anything you've got."

The fire marshal shook his head. "He was wearing a hoodie, and his face was turned away from me when I saw him leaning into the wall. I went to confront him, but he dropped the board and took off like a jackrabbit. Practically knocked a homeless man to the ground, too."

"The homeless man—six feet tall, red beard and brown hair?" Rick asked.

"Yeah, that fits. He was over by the furniture store's loading dock for a moment and then he disappeared down the far end of the alley," Medina said.

"Thanks for everything," Rick answered.

"You're through here, I assume?" Medina asked.

"For now," Rick said, then added, "Would you and your men keep an eye out for a gold crucifix on a chain? The male server who worked here last night—Crawford—was hanging around when we first arrived. He claimed he lost it last night and came back to look around."

"We can do that."

Rick hurried with Kim back to his SUV. "I'm going to drive around to see if I can spot Mike."

"I'll help you look."

After twenty minutes of Rick circling downtown and driving down alleys, he glanced over at her, shaking his head. "It's like he vanished off the face of the earth."

"Mike's like that," she said. "I've tried to help him, get him connected with people who'll give him food and shelter, but he didn't want any part of it. He sets his own rules and comes and goes as he pleases."

"There's something to be said for that, I suppose."

"There's one thing I'm sure about. If he knew someone was out to hurt me, Mike would find a way to let me know. He's not a bad guy. He's hiding—from the world, from himself, I just don't know—but there's a lot of good inside him."

"And you know this how?" Maybe Kim was still an innocent, a woman determined to see the best in everyone.

"I'm not just another idealistic do-gooder, if that's what you're thinking," she said. "One time after I handed him a sack of food, I reached into my purse and my wallet fell out. It was late, I was in a rush and I didn't discover it missing until I was finally home."

"Did you have cash in it?" he asked.

"Oh, yeah. My salary, my tips and my one credit card. I canceled the card, but my driver's license was also gone. Replacing it and buying groceries for the week was going to be difficult without any cash."

"Couldn't you have asked your uncle for help?" he asked. "Or at least for an advance on your salary?"

She shook her head. "I wouldn't have done that until I'd exhausted every other option."

He bit back a grin. He was the same way.

"The next afternoon when I went back to the Brickhouse to start my shift, Mike met me by the back door and handed me my wallet. He'd kept it safe for me. I tried to give him some money as a reward, but he wouldn't take it. He just asked that I bring him a *sopaipilla* with green chili for dinner—but only if I wouldn't get into trouble. That's the only time he ever spoke to me in full sentences."

Rick smiled, glad to see she'd made a logical decision, not one based on pity, an emotion that often conspired against a man, destroying him from the inside out.

To this day, he still remembered the pity he'd seen in almost everyone's eyes after his mother had abandoned him at six years old at the trading post. Those looks had completely sapped his confidence, continually reminding him that no matter how sorry they felt, few would ever open their doors to him. They had their own lives, and he wasn't included.

Last year, after surviving the knife fight, he'd wondered if the scar on his face would arouse a similar reaction. He'd made it a point to carry himself ramrod-straight, determined not to give anyone an occasion to feel sorry for him.

As it turned out, the agents he'd been working with had looked at the scar as a badge of honor and respected it. Outside the Bureau he'd held his head high, went about his business without hesitation, and in the end his efforts paid off. He'd seen fear in some and shock in others, but pity had been absent.

"I know we were supposed to go to Turquoise Dreams, but do you mind if we stop by my place first? I live in a duplex that's on the way and I'd like to drop off my books and notes. I also want to make sure that the mail carrier picked up a job application I left in the PO box."

"What kind of job are you applying for?" he asked as he followed directions to her home.

"One that's connected to law enforcement," she said, crossing her fingers. "There's a security company in town that hires and trains, and it would give me the kind of experience that could come in handy when I apply for the police academy."

He glanced at her quickly. "Exactly what position are you applying for?"

"The only part-time they've got at Complete Security right now—monitoring cameras at night. There's more to it, but they're very tight-lipped and don't give out job details until after they do a background check."

"How's the pay?" he asked, knowing they were talking about his brother Daniel's firm. Level One Security was the parent company of Complete Security, a new venture for his brother. CS was an electronic service Daniel had started up for small businesses in the area.

"The pay's just average, but they could really

teach me a lot—if I get the job." She pointed. "Here we are, up ahead on the right, 1916 Pine Street."

Seeing the For Rent sign, he tensed. "The other side of the duplex is empty?" he asked, not liking the tactical complications that presented.

"Not for long. The rent's reasonable and the owner advertises on campus."

He quickly parked. As he got out of the SUV, the hairs at the back of his neck prickled. Something was wrong, he could feel it.

Rick looked around, but everything appeared peaceful.

As they stepped onto her small porch, he noticed that her door was slightly ajar. "Do you have a housekeeper or a nosey landlord?"

"A housekeeper? Me?" Kim laughed and then, following his gaze, saw what he was looking at. "I always lock it before I leave, but my landlord, Mr. Hopson, has a set of keys. That might be him, replacing the furnace filter," she said. "Come in. I'll introduce you."

"No." He pulled her back. "Wait outside."

She froze. "What did you see?"

Rick reached for the pistol inside his boot, then moved forward quietly, holding the weapon down by his side, the safety now off.

Chapter Six

Rick pushed the door back hard, to make sure no one was hiding behind it, then went in. At a glance it was obvious there'd been a break-in. An older model TV had been dumped off its stand and kicked in, and ceramic figures and books had been swept off the shelves. It was difficult to say if Kim had been robbed or if this had been the work of vandals.

He searched each room, moving carefully, but the intruder was nowhere around so he put away his weapon. An open bedroom window and a footprint on the dresser beneath it showed how the intruder had gained entry. Pulling out his cell phone, he called Preston and reported the break-in. He then walked back to Kim, who was standing in the doorway, looking inside as she shook her head in obvious disgust.

Rick waved her inside. "Brace yourself, it's like this everywhere," he advised. "And put on those gloves Preston gave you before you touch anything."

She stepped inside, pulling on one of the gloves, and cursed aloud. Basically everything that had been on the shelves was now on the floor.

Looking through the doorway she could see the kitchen was a mess, too. All the chairs had been overturned and every drawer upended.

When she walked into the bedroom, she discovered that the futon had been sliced down the middle with something sharp, like a box cutter. "Why would anyone do this to me?"

"It looks like they might have been looking for something."

"Hidden inside a cheap mattress that was completely intact?" She shook her head. "No, this was done to hurt me."

"Hey," he said, gently pulling her into his arms.

He liked the way Kim fit against him. She was soft and warm. He pressed his lips to her forehead and then, as she looked up, he kissed her.

She melted against him with a sigh and parted her lips.

That was one invitation he couldn't refuse. For those precious seconds, nothing existed except her and him. He caught the scent of wildflowers—her shampoo, or maybe her perfume.

She was sweet, yet passionate, and he loved the way she clung to him. He'd only wanted to comfort her, but other infinitely darker needs soon rose inside him. Knowing he might lose control if he didn't release her, he forced himself to step back. "It'll be okay, Kim. Don't let them get to you."

Kim stepped back as well, and took a long look around the room. "The bed…" she said at last, avoiding his eyes. "I need to try to save the mattress. I can't afford to replace it. Could you hold the two torn sides together while I sew them up?"

Pulling on his latex gloves, Rick went over to help her, but as he brought the two sides of the slashed canvas together, he felt something hard underneath the surface in the bedding material. "There's something in here." Putting his gloved hand inside, he pulled out a bone about six inches long.

"What the heck is that?" she asked.

Rick cursed under his breath. "Do you have a paper or plastic bag?" he asked. "We need to turn this over to Preston."

She ran to the kitchen, then hurried back. "You think that could be a human bone?"

"Maybe. The lab'll tell us more."

"This sure has the earmarks of Angelina's skin-walker stuff."

He looked at her quickly. "Say again?"

"Angelina never became a medicine woman. She said she found something more useful. She claimed she could put a curse on just about anybody who deserved one."

"She *admitted* she's a skinwalker?" Rick asked,

surprised. Even if she had become one somewhere along the way, it seemed unlikely she'd let anyone know. Witches were despised among The People, and the evil ones, as they were often described, kept their practices a secret.

"She didn't say it in so many words. She just mentioned that she found the opposite of a medicine woman—a skinwalker—much more interesting. She said their ways were more practical," Kim explained. "I don't believe in stuff like that, so I never paid much attention."

"So maybe the break-in was someone's way of warning you to stay away from me," Rick said.

"Angelina's already fired me. She has no more say in my life. Whoever did this is just plain mean."

"Even if you don't believe in Navajo witchcraft, the people who choose to practice it are usually unbalanced," Rick said. "The further into the practice they get, the more likely they are to get out of control."

"From what I've seen, Angelina's all talk. She wants people to fear her, but it'll take more than a bone and a dead spider to scare me," she said.

"She pulled a gun on me today," Rick reminded her.

Kim nodded slowly. "That's in another class entirely."

"Since you're interested in police work and need a job, I have a suggestion. I've been away from

Hartley for years, so you know the community better than I do. I could use your help," Rick said.

"Does that mean you want to hire me?" she asked, surprised.

"In a way. With your permission, I'd like to talk to Daniel. In case you didn't know, Level One Security is Complete Security's parent company—and my brother owns and controls both. Maybe you can become a paid intern and work with me. I can teach you investigative techniques. In return for the training and job, you could agree to stay with the company for at least a year at the same salary. If I can pull this off, how does that sound?"

"I won't be earning my degree for at least another eighteen months, so it sounds perfect. I'd gladly work for your brother for a year. Having been employed by a company like his will look great on my résumé."

"Okay, then." He went to the window and glanced outside. "It looks like Preston and some of his officers are here. While you fill him in and show him around, I'll give Daniel a call."

While Preston spoke to Kim, Rick moved away to call his brother, telling Daniel what he had in mind.

"So what do you think?"

"I've done that before for people with potential, so it's fine, but there's something I need to know.

Is she getting under your skin? Is that why you're doing this?"

"No, it's not that. I was the reason she lost her job. It was unintentional, but it's a fact."

"As logical as it sounds, my gut tells me there's more to it," Daniel replied.

Rick ended the call just as Kim and Preston came over to talk to him. From their expressions, he could tell something else was wrong.

"What's up, guys?" Rick asked.

"In a normal break-in we'd have dozens of usable prints, but this place was wiped clean. The only prints we found were on the lock and the door itself, which makes me think they belong to you and Kim."

"That settles it. This was no ordinary burglary or act of vandalism," Rick said somberly.

"I'd advise you not to stay here," Preston told Kim. "It's no longer safe."

"I have no other place to go. I can't stay with a friend or relative and put them in danger, too, nor do I have money for a motel."

"There might be a way of getting around that problem," Rick said, pulling out his phone. "But I'll need to check something out first. Excuse me for a minute," he added, then stepped outside.

Rick returned a short time later. "My brother Kyle and his wife, Erin, are willing to give you a room at the family home in Copper Canyon. It's northwest of Shiprock, on the Rez. Except for last night, when I didn't want to add a long drive to my evening, I'm staying there, as well. I can drive us back and forth."

"I don't know.... I hate to intrude," Kim said.

"We're going to be working together, so that'll make it simpler all the way around," Rick said.

Rick noted the pleased look on Kim's face and the surprise on Preston's.

"It's a logical solution," Rick added.

"How soon do you want to leave?" Kim asked.

"As soon as you're ready. So go pack what you'll need."

"Not so fast. Let's take one last look around," Preston said.

Rick's eyes narrowed. "You think you missed something?"

Preston nodded slowly. "Yeah, call it cop's instinct."

"Is it still okay if I pack a few personal things while we look around?" she asked Preston, who nodded.

In her bedroom, the two men waited as Kim placed her laptop in her suitcase and then opened the dresser drawer. As she began to remove essential clothing, something fell to the floor.

"Drop a button?" Rick said, bending to look. "I guess not," he added, picking up the curious-looking object with a gloved hand and holding it up for Preston to see.

"What on earth is that?" Kim asked. "A… tooth?"

"A *long, hollow* tooth," Rick observed. "Like a rattler's fang."

"Does that have any special significance?" Kim asked. "Other than the obvious?"

"According to our creation stories, witchcraft started before mankind emerged from the earth. First Woman passed it out to the others, but Snake didn't have pockets, so he took it in his mouth. That's why snake bites can kill," Preston explained.

She shuddered. "Sorry, but I don't think that was meant for me. If you hadn't explained, I wouldn't have known, and the point would have been lost. This was left for you guys," she said, looking at Rick, then Preston.

They exchanged glances before Rick nodded to his brother, who bagged and tagged the evidence.

SEVERAL MINUTES LATER, after signing the required incident report statements, Rick and Kim drove southwest through downtown Hartley.

"The incidents we've seen so far don't make a lot of sense if you put them together," Kim commented. "No one motive seems to fit. What we saw at my place was a result of creepy maliciousness. What happened at the Brickhouse was attempted mass murder. One was intended to scare, the other to kill. If the same person was responsible, you'd think the sequence of events would have been reversed. We may be dealing with multiple suspects."

He nodded slowly. "Solid deduction."

Kim glanced around. "Heading out of town in this direction will take us past the hospital. Can we stop there for a few moments so I can visit my uncle?"

"Yeah. In fact, that's a good idea," Rick said. "Are you two close?"

"He was there for me when my dad died, but Uncle Frank's not someone who invited a girl's confidences. Nor is he the huggy-kissy type at all," she said with a wry smile. "Dad's brother is a man's man. I'm sure he'll come through this— and just as sure that he'll never talk about it again."

"Is he financially secure enough to weather what happened at the tavern?"

"Yeah, the place was well insured. As long as he can reopen the restaurant, he'll be fine, but I bet he's glad he didn't actually buy his partner out as he'd planned."

"Arthur Johnson, right?" Rick asked and saw her nod. "What can you tell me about him?"

"He and my uncle go way back. Art's wife got sick a few years ago, and although they had health insurance, there were a lot of deductibles and collateral expenses that nearly bankrupted him. After she died, he sold almost everything he owned except his share of the Brickhouse," she explained. "I think Art kept it mostly because of my uncle."

"How involved is Johnson in running the Brickhouse?" Rick asked.

"Art's a silent partner all the way—always signing off on Uncle Frank's operating decisions without question."

"He hasn't showed up on the scene yet, so I'm guessing Arthur doesn't live in Hartley?"

"No, he doesn't. Art's got a rustic cabin he just loves for some odd reason. It's in the Sangre de Cristo Mountains above Santa Fe."

Rick pulled into the hospital parking lot and glanced across the street to the west. There were several businesses there, including a few small warehouses and a low block building with a big sign.

"Turquoise Dreams. Isn't that Angelina's other shop?"

"Yes, and we can go over afterward, providing Angelina's pickup isn't still there," she said, pointing to the vehicle on the east side with a custom license plate that read *'lina.*

They entered the hospital, officially a regional medical center, and stopped at the front desk. After a short wait they were directed to Frank Nelson's room. He was alone in the semiprivate room, watching TV.

Frank looked over at them as they entered and smiled. "Good to see you two! I've been hoping for some news. Is the restaurant a total loss?"

"Pretty much," Kim said with a nod. "We'll have to file a claim with the insurance company as soon as the fire marshal has completed his preliminary investigation. There'll probably be some delays because it was clearly arson."

"That place was all I had," Frank muttered. "Who would have done something like that?"

"You co-own the Brickhouse Tavern with Arthur Johnson, I understand," Rick mentioned off hand, hoping to start a conversation.

"Yeah, and I have to let him know what's happened. Unfortunately he's probably still out of reach. He left on one of his late-season fishing trips a few days ago, out of state, I think. Art likes to hike deep into the mountains, going to places where he can't be reached except on foot or horseback. I know he's still grieving for his wife," he said, his voice heavy. "He'll call me when he's available again."

"Any idea when that'll be?" Rick asked.

"A few more days, maybe a week, depending on the fishing. Art doesn't have to answer to anyone these days."

"I understand that the restaurant was doing well," Rick said.

"Oh, yeah. We have a lot of loyal customers and

always manage to stay in the black. The insurance won't be enough to cover all the losses, though, just in case you're thinking along those lines."

"Will you reopen?" Rick asked.

"I guess it'll depend on my partner. Art might want to just take his share of the insurance settlement and walk. I'll do my best to talk him out of it, of course, because I love that place."

"Has there ever been any bad blood between you and Angelina Curley?" Rick asked, and to his surprise, Frank barked out a laugh.

"That lunatic? The woman's nuts, but at least she doesn't mess with me. Your foster father and I were friends, and he gave me a leather pouch with flint arrowheads, corn pollen and some other items he referred to as medicine. They were supposed to work together to keep evil at bay. I showed it to her once when she was complaining about some parking meters I was pushing the town council to approve. I don't know if that was what did it, but ever since then, she's kept her distance."

Kim stepped closer to the bed. "Uncle Frank, I came by to tell you that I won't be at my place for a while," she said, explaining about the break-in.

"She'll be safe where I'm taking her," Rick added.

"Aren't there any surveillance cameras around your duplex? I don't recall seeing any, but what about the street side?" Frank asked.

She shook her head. "It's a low crime neighborhood except for the usual college parties that can get a bit loud. Anyone who lives on my block is too busy getting by, Uncle Frank. Not much to steal."

"My brother will canvas the neighborhood and check out traffic cameras," Rick said as they readied to leave.

"I'll be out of the hospital in a day or so and be able to take a look at what's left of my restaurant," Frank said. "If you need me, Kim, call my cell phone number."

Outside in the parking lot a few minutes later, Rick noted that Angelina's pickup was still parked in front of the jewelry store. "Looks like we'll have to come back later," he said, nodding across the street.

"You're right. There's no sense in another confrontation right now," Kim replied, climbing into the passenger side of the SUV.

Once they were on their way again, Kim glanced at Rick. "From the questions you asked my uncle, I gather you're thinking that this could be a case of insurance fraud. Since my uncle was struck on the head and left to die, he can't be a suspect. So that leaves whom? Art?"

"He's one possibility. Preston's people will check the evidence and then we'll see where we stand. Patience is the key."

"Sorry, I'm fresh out."

AN HOUR LATER they'd left the wide river valley far behind them, and were well on their way into the Navajo Nation. The dry mesas were scattered in the distance, those to the north and west topped by junipers and piñons. Beyond those formations were the foothills, leading to mountain ranges and forests filled with pines and fir.

"I love this open country. It's not houses backed up against houses. The skies are blue and you can breathe out here."

"I gather you're a country girl at heart?"

"No, I belong in a town or small city, hopefully wearing a badge someday. To me, coming out here is a chance to decompress. Everyone needs that." She saw the flicker of approval that played on his features. "Is that why you're staying at Copper Canyon?"

"Yeah. The place is small but it's a three-bedroom. Kyle and Erin invited me to stay with them until I could figure out what was next for me."

As they drew closer to their destination, a high mesa that curved into a blind canyon with a single outlet at the base, he smiled.

"This is Copper Canyon—home. My brothers and I know this place like the backs of our hands."

She glanced around, a worried frown on her face. "It's really isolated here, Rick."

"This is the safest spot around. There's only one way in for vehicles—a narrow road easily monitored. We're on it now. Also the place transmits sound like a giant megaphone. From the moment we crossed the wooden bridge, Kyle and Erin could hear the rattle of the timbers even though the ranch house is still some distance away."

"I don't see a house anywhere," she said, looking around.

"It's farther ahead. Maybe a quarter of a mile."

"From what I can see, there's a series of trails. That means there has to be more than one route to the ranch house once you're inside the canyon," she said, observing her surroundings. "This particular pathway is super rough," she said, holding on to the armrest as the SUV rocked from side to side. "How about taking the one to our left?"

"That's a common mistake, and a bad idea. The other trails may look smoother, and people who haven't been here before often choose those, which explain their presence. Before long, those people either get bogged down or high center their vehicle," he said. "There's also an arroyo ahead that intersects the other routes. That'll stop anyone not on horseback or foot."

She looked around her. "I see what looks like a big, plowed field, but other than that the trees and undergrowth are pretty thick. I've already seen rabbits and quail. Is there any other wildlife around?"

"Big cats occasionally hunt here, and so do coyotes. Then there's the occasional bear that comes down out of the mountains. But the bigger predators avoid people. The trick is never to corner them."

Kim soon spotted the rectangular, sand-colored, stucco-and-wood-framed house, not far from one of the steepest cliffs. The metal roof shimmered in the sunlight. Beyond that she noted the log corral with two beautiful piebald horses.

"Horses!"

"Women and horses," he said, smiling. "Those belong to Kyle and his wife. She fell in love with them from the moment she saw them at Gene's ranch," he said. Then pointing ahead, he added, "Looks like Erin's just finished feeding them."

Kim saw a petite brunette brushing hay from her clothes as she walked toward the house.

As Rick pulled up and parked by the side of the house, a short distance from a small storage shed, his brother came out the back door to greet them.

"Welcome, guys," Kyle said.

"So you heard us coming?" Rick asked with a grin.

"Yes, but only a few minutes ago. I'm not as good as Gene and Preston at picking up visitors at long range."

"Yeah, you and me both," he answered and looked at Kim. "Some of my brothers are incredibly attuned to nature here. For example, the absence of birds or their sudden flight lets them know when anyone's around. Gene, in particular, can listen to a coyote's howl and tell you if everything is okay."

Erin joined them and gave Kim a hug, having first met her at the Brickhouse. "You'll be safe and comfortable here, Kim. Come inside and help me fix dinner."

As they reached the small porch, Kim heard an ominous rumble. Looking off into the distance, she noted the billowing clouds beyond the canyon walls to the west.

Rick followed her gaze and glanced at his brother. "White Thunder. Remember what Hosteen Silver used to say about him?"

Kyle nodded. "None of the medicine men ever called on White Thunder during ceremonies because it was said he only brought trouble."

"So that's a bad sign?" Kim asked.

Rick shook his head. "Not necessarily. Thunders have the power to find things, too."

They'd just reached the front door when a silver-gray hawk cried overhead and landed in a tall piñon about a hundred feet from the house. It remained there, gazing down at them.

"Isn't it beautiful? It hangs around here a lot," Erin whispered.

"Hosteen Silver's spiritual brother was Winter Hawk," Rick told Kim.

Kyle nodded slowly. "White Thunder and now Winter Hawk.... It's a welcome and a warning."

"Well, if there's danger ahead, Copper Canyon's the place to be. Let's go inside," Rick said, his voice tense.

Chapter Seven

Kim felt Rick's tension as clearly as her own. She didn't believe in omens, but she didn't dismiss them outright, either. She'd learned at an early age that New Mexico was the land of the unexplained. Here, the mysterious existed along with the ordinary, each finding its own place.

As she stepped inside the main room, she smiled, feeling instantly comfortable. It looked like the interior of a rustic cabin, very similar to those in country magazines. Though sparsely decorated, it had an undeniable elegance.

To her right the room opened up and against the far wall was the kitchen. Closer, and in the center of that space, was a large dining table pieced from several pine logs.

Centered in the room was a sofa covered in rich brown leather. Beautiful wool Navajo rugs were hung on the wall opposite a huge stone fireplace with vents that probably circulated the warm air generated from the fire.

On the wall opposite the dining side was a walk-in closet that had been converted to fit either computer equipment or TV screens.

"What a special place!" she told Erin. "I can see why you wanted to live here."

"The brothers all agreed that we could make it our home, so I sold my place in Hartley and Kyle and I moved in," Erin explained. "It's the perfect place for us. I can irrigate and have more land to grow my crops. The fields have already been leveled, and this coming spring we'll be putting in rabbit-proof fencing. I'm a chili farmer and Kyle's in the family security business. He runs Complete Security for Daniel and often works from home."

Kim smiled. "I work for Complete Security now, too, as a paid intern."

"I've heard," Erin replied, leading the way to the kitchen. Rick and Kyle were already there, coffee mugs in hand.

"It's hot and it'll warm you up," Rick said. "Want a cup?"

"It's *hot*? That's the nicest thing you can say about my coffee?" Erin said, laughing as she handed Kim a mug.

Sipping her coffee, Kim watched them kid around with each other as they all pitched in to fix dinner. Although the fare was simple, she had to admit the green chili hamburger, thick and on homemade buns, was the best she'd ever tasted.

After dinner, they retreated to the sofa and chairs. The blazing fireplace would keep them warm and comfortable. "Your letter, the one Hosteen Silver left for you, is on the third shelf of the bookcase," Kyle said to Rick.

"Although I'm tempted not to read it, that would be showing disrespect, and I owe Hosteen Silver everything," Rick said, walking over to pick it up. They'd all been left letters to read upon their foster father's death, but Rick's undercover work had kept him away. This was the first time he'd ever even seen the envelope.

"We've all read ours, so yours is the last," Kyle said.

Rick sat on the hearth and stared at the envelope in his hand.

"The longer you put it off, the harder it'll get," Kim warned softly.

Rick tore open the sealed envelope, his expression hard. In a gesture of solidarity, Kyle came over to stand beside his brother as Rick pulled out the small piece of paper.

No one spoke as Rick read it silently. "As cryptic as ever," he said at last, then read it out loud. "'It's not Eagle's nature to accept what seems to be. As what is hidden comes to light, your fight will begin. You will walk in beauty only after blue overcomes red and your eyes are opened to a truth that eluded me.'" Rick placed the paper on the coffee table so they could all see.

"There's something different about your letter, bro," Kyle said. "First, it doesn't really look like Hosteen Silver's handwriting. It's shaky. Then look at the date on top. That's the same day we think Hosteen Silver disappeared."

Rick took a closer look at the letter. "It's his writing. Look at the *f* with that extra loop in its center. The *g* is also not connected to the letter following it." After a moment Rick added, "I'm guessing his hand was trembling."

"The man was without fear. Maybe he was sick at the time he wrote it," Kyle said.

"That's what I think, too," Rick answered.

"What's that stuff about blue overcoming red?" Kyle asked. "It sounds vaguely familiar, but I can't nail it down."

"It's part of the story Hosteen Silver used to tell us about the Hero Twins and their special prayer stick."

"Who were the Hero Twins?" Kim asked.

"Navajo creation stories tell us about the sons of Changing Woman and Sun. The twins were great warriors, so their father, Sun, sent them on a great quest to destroy mankind's enemies. Before they left, they were given a special prayer stick that was covered with blue paint and sparkling earth, symbols of peace and happiness. They were told that anytime the prayer stick turned red, a deadly battle lay ahead."

Kyle nodded. "Now I remember."

"I think he was telling me that there's a mission I have to complete here, a wrong I have to right before I can find peace," Rick said.

"But if he didn't tell you, how will you know what that wrong is?" Kim asked.

"That's the essence of all of Hosteen Silver's predictions," Rick answered. "You don't have to go looking for answers. Eventually what you're after, or what you need, will come to you."

After the revelation, everyone's mood turned somber. Although they remained by the fireplace for several more hours, they were quiet for the most part, all lost in their own thoughts.

Finally, Erin stood and stretched. "I'm going to bed. I can show you your room if you like, Kim."

"Tonight I want to keep a lookout, so I'll be sleeping on the sofa," Rick said.

"How about we trade off keeping watch? You could crash in the remaining bedroom when I'm on duty," Kyle said. "We've got cameras rigged up at a few key points, too, so we'll get an alert the minute anything larger than a coyote comes down the road or approaches the house. The system immediately starts to record, too, so just open the cabinet and check the monitors if we get a hit."

"Works for me," Rick said. "I'll take the first watch and wake you up in four hours."

"I could help," Kim said. "I'm a good observer. Right now I can tell no one's around. There's a coyote howling in the distance, and I don't think it would announce its presence if humans were around."

Kyle smiled. "No one ever hears Rick move— not unless he wants you to, that is. We used to call him Shadowman."

Rick smiled. "It's a gift."

"You said you'd train me, and here I am. Let me help," she insisted.

"All right," Rick said at last. "Neither of us got much sleep last night, but together we can keep each other alert." Rick looked at his brother. "I'll come get you when it's time."

When Kyle and Erin left, Rick turned off all the lights. Only the glow from burning piñon logs in the fireplace—and the monitors—illuminated the room. "I'm glad you volunteered to stay up. I'm tired and it'll be easier to stay focused with a partner."

She smiled, glad to be considered a partner. "Tell me more about that note," she said, taking a seat on the hearth. "If I read you right, there was something else about it that troubled you."

He nodded slowly. "My gut's telling me that Hosteen Silver wrote that after he knew he was dying. Since I'm the youngest, he probably put me last on the list when it came to his final message. I think that's why his handwriting was so shaky," he said. "I know Hosteen Silver was trying to tell me something, but he always overestimated my ability to understand him."

"I have a feeling he knew exactly what he was doing when he deliberately chose you to do what needed to be done," Kim said. Rick could be gentle, but his strength never wavered. Remembering the way he'd kissed her, she felt her skin prickle. "How are you different from your brothers?" she added, forcing herself to focus on the conversation.

"They prefer team efforts, but I like working solo. That's why I volunteered for undercover work." He stood by the side of the window, pulling back the heavy curtain to look out into the canyon. The desert was bathed in moonlight and every rock and patch of open ground wore a faint, glowing blanket.

"You're fine working with your brothers, though," she said.

"That's because I trust them, but I still like taking point."

"Wow, talk about double-speak. Or is it ego?"

He chuckled. "Maybe both." He walked to the note Hosteen Silver had left for him, picked it up off the table, folded it and placed it in his back pocket.

"What I don't understand is the reference to Eagle. Who or what is he?" Kim asked.

"That's also linked to our Traditionalist beliefs. Hosteen Silver gave each of us a special fetish, and mine's Eagle. The spirit of the animal is said to become one with its owner, and by sharing its special qualities, it enhances my own."

"You mean you can see things that are far away?" Kim asked, trying to understand.

"No, it's not like that. Eagle stands for vision and power through balance. It's not distance vision, however, it's the ability to see the overall picture, something any investigator has to learn to do." As he checked the monitors, he added, "Eagle's about honoring knowledge by knowing when it's okay to share it and when it's better to withhold it."

"Sometimes I get so sidetracked by details, I lose the overall perspective. I wish I had Eagle's ability to see the whole picture." Kim took a deep breath. "When I lost my job at Angelina's I was terrified. Having my apartment wrecked after that made things even worse.

"Now that I have a new perspective," she added, "I realize that getting fired from Silver Heritage was one of the best things that ever happened to me."

"Angelina made it that tough?"

She nodded. "I liked to take time to talk to the customers, to get a feel for what they were really looking for, but Angelina was all about making the sale—" She stopped abruptly and her eyes widened. "I just recalled something that may be important."

Rick nodded. "Go on."

"About three weeks ago there was a curious incident at the store. An Anglo man in his late forties came in. He was a professor at a college in Durango. He asked if we could connect him to a local Navajo medicine man who was said to occasionally use Hopi fetishes in blessings for protection."

"Did he mention Hosteen Silver by name?"

"No, but I was sure that's who he meant, so I suggested he speak to Angelina. At the time, I didn't know about the bad blood between her and Hosteen Silver. The instant I mentioned her by name, the professor politely declined and left the store. That's the last time I saw him."

"You don't have a name?"

"Sorry. I never asked, but I'd recognize him if I saw him again. If he's still teaching up in Durango, there's got to be a photo of him somewhere."

"Good thinking. We'll look that up in the morning."

They kept each other alert until 2:00 a.m. when Kyle came into the room, unannounced.

Rick grinned. "So I see your internal clock is still working."

"Go to sleep, you two," Kyle said, ushering them out. "You'll have a long day tomorrow."

Rick walked Kim to her bedroom. "Sleep well."

"You going to be in the next bedroom, Rick?" she asked.

"Nah, I'll crawl into a sleeping bag in front of the fireplace. I prefer to be on hand in case Kyle needs me."

She went inside the room and, exhausted, stripped down to her underwear and crawled in between the heavy blankets. Almost as soon as her head hit the pillow, she was fast asleep.

Kim never woke until the sun peered through the curtains, yet it wasn't the daylight that had nudged her awake. Unsure of what it was, she went to the window and peered out.

It was dawn, but the canyon floor was still in shade because of the cliffs. Rick was already outside. She saw him check the immediate area, including the shed beside the house, then head up the canyon.

Curious, she dressed quickly then went into the living room. It was empty. Kyle had gone back to bed. Making an impromptu decision, Kim slipped out the front door. Being Rick's backup was part of her job now.

Bundling her coat around her tightly, and trying to protect herself from the cold breeze, she followed the trail Rick's boots left in the sand.

Chapter Eight

Rick looked up at the pine trees dotting the top of the mesa. They glowed in the sunlight that had yet to penetrate to the desert floor. The cliffs were layered top to bottom in a kaleidoscope of color, from yellow-orange to a pale cranberry-red that turned purple above the shadow line. It was more beautiful here than he remembered.

This was his turf, but he still didn't feel at home. Maybe he just needed to reconnect. He jammed his hands inside his leather jacket and continued walking.

Every day at this time Hosteen Silver would leave the ranch house to go offer his prayers to Dawn at a spot high atop the sandstone bedrock. His voice, filled with power and conviction, would echo in the walls of the narrow canyon.

Without charting a course, Rick moved farther up slope, deep into Copper Canyon.

It was here that he'd heard his foster father cry to the morning sky, *"Hozhone nas clee, hozhone nas clee,"* which translated meant "Now all is well, now all is well." Then he'd scatter pollen from his medicine bag as an offering to Dawn, so he could continue to walk in beauty.

Memories crowded Rick's mind as he stared into the brightening cliff wall to his left. That's when he remembered the other reason he'd come this way as a boy. Hearing the spring-fed creek that ran the length of the canyon year round, he smiled.

As his brothers before him, he'd staked out his own special place, one too private to share. Although his brothers' spots were soon known to the rest of the family, no one had ever discovered his.

He smiled, wondering if his sole treasure still lay nestled in that hole carved into the rock face, hidden by the thick spread of junipers that scented the air year-round. There was a gap in the cliffs here, one cleverly hidden from the curious by nature herself.

Rick stepped around the tall rock that seemingly blocked further passage. Pressing his way sideways between the plants that formed a natural barrier, he walked up a rabbit trail that was almost obscured by permanent shadows.

He never would have found this place as a boy, as a matter of fact, if he hadn't seen a cottontail disappear into the cliff side. About twenty steps into the narrow opening, which closed off completely just around the curve, he stopped and searched for the familiar crevice created by the splitting of a sandstone layer centuries ago.

He'd just reached in when he heard footsteps—not animal. He spun in a crouch instantly, gun in hand.

"Whoa! It's me," Kim said, hands up in the air.

"You followed me?" he asked, surprised. No one had ever been able to do that before. But then, he'd been on a walk, not trying to evade the enemy.

"Yes, I'm supposed to be your backup. That's part of my training, too. What if you ran into danger?"

"If I had, what could you have done? You're not armed."

"I can fight. I was deployed in Afghanistan as a cargo specialist," she said. "And I'm armed, not with a gun, but with this," she said, holding up a can of Mace.

He smiled. "What they sell as Mace these days is usually just pepper spray. Anyone who's drugged up or has any training won't be deterred by that."

"I wasn't thinking that you'd run into humans. I was thinking more of wild animals."

"I'm armed," he said, putting his pistol away.

"What if you'd fallen off a cliff or stepped on a rattler?"

He decided not to argue the point. Her motives had been right on target, but he was curious how she'd pulled it off. "I know you didn't follow me from the house, not visually. I'd have seen you."

"Tracks," she said, pointing to the sandy earth. "I learned it at Boy Scouts. Actually, I had a friend who was a Boy Scout and he'd teach me what he was learning. It was far more interesting that what my Girl Scout troop was doing."

He laughed. "Yeah, that fits you."

"So why are you out here?" she said, changing the subject.

He grew serious. "I was trying to reconnect with the place I called home for so many years. This was my special spot. When I first arrived at Copper Canyon, after Hosteen Silver convinced family services that I wasn't beyond hope and took me in—as he had before with my foster brothers—I went hiking a lot. One day I found an arrowhead. It wasn't particularly valuable, but I chose to see it as something this place had meant for me to find. It fit the image I had of myself back then—a survivor and a fighter."

"You still are," she said softly.

"Yes, I'm that—and more," he said. Parting some branches, he reached into the shallow crevice in the sandstone wall. "Let's see if my arrowhead is still…" He paused for a moment. "There's something else back here."

He pulled out a pocket-size, metal breath-mint box containing the arrowhead and, along with it, a small, spiral notebook enclosed in a plastic freezer bag.

Curious, Rick put the box that held the arrowhead back for a moment, then opened the plastic bag and took out the notebook. Inside, on each page, were ink drawings. "The Plant People."

"Who are they?" she said, trying to get a closer look at the drawings.

"A Traditionalist Navajo believes our native plants are people who go where they will, and can harm or bless, depending on how you appeal to them," he said. "These particular ones are the plants Hosteen Silver used for his ceremonies... but look at the top of the page. That's some kind of code."

"Do you recognize it?"

"No, but he obviously left this here for me, so he thought I'd be able to decipher and read it." He studied it for a moment longer.

"This was your special hiding place, but you shared the location with Hosteen Silver?"

"No, but it doesn't surprise me that he knew," Rick said. He held the notebook and leafed through its pages again. "I think there's a good chance that he left this here for me the same day he went for his final walk into the desert. The numbers that make up the code are shaky, like the handwriting in his note to me."

"I don't understand," Kim admitted. "Why

would your father just walk off like that to die? Why not pass away in his house or call 9-1-1 and get help?"

"That's not the way of a Traditionalist Navajo," he said, his voice heavy. "Had he passed away at home, many would have believed that the ranch house would have drawn his *chindi* and become cursed."

"You mean by his ghost?"

"No, the *chindi* is not a man's spirit. It's only the evil side of him that has to remain earthbound because it can't unite with universal harmony."

"Do you and your brothers believe in the *chindi?*"

"No, not really, we're all Modernists. But like most Navajos, we still respect the old ways," he said. "The things I've seen on the Rez, and what I've learned from our Traditionalists, have taught me that there's a lot more to life that what we see and can easily explain."

"Listen. I hear a voice," Kim said.

It was Kyle, yelling for Rick.

Rick yelled back. "We're okay." He glanced at Kim. "It's time to head back, but there's something I need to do first."

He took the arrowhead out of the mint box and placed it in his pocket. Then, using his cell phone, he photographed each page of the notebook, enclosed it in the plastic bag and placed it back in the crevice.

"Why are you leaving it here?" she asked.

"My foster father hadn't been suffering from any obvious terminal disease. It's impossible that my brothers, and the people who lived in the area and saw him often, would have missed something that important. Whatever caused him to walk off and die like that came on very suddenly.

"Over the past several months we've all begun to think it's possible that he was murdered—maybe by some toxic substance, or more likely, a plant-derived poison that wasn't detected until too late. That would explain why he left this documentation of the Plant People. The notebook may be the single most important clue we have. If I take it with me, and people come after us, I risk losing or damaging it," Rick said. "The notebook has remained safe here all this time. For now, this is where it should stay."

"Will you tell your brothers?" Kim asked.

"Yeah, and as soon as I can I'll send Daniel and Paul the pages. Both of them are good at breaking codes."

"We're heading back to Hartley this morning, then?"

"Yes, but on the way back to the ranch house we need to rub out our tracks. I trust my brothers, of course, and you, but I want to make sure no one else who comes into the canyon can track us here," he said.

Rick broke off a juniper branch and showed her how to erase obvious marks in the sand left by their shoes. "Carefully scoop up handfuls of sand, smooth over those scoop marks, then scatter the sand lightly over the trail the branch leaves as I run it over the ground. Just don't pour the sand onto any leaves if you can help it."

It took them several minutes to finish the job around the cliff exterior, but the rest was easy. They were back at the ranch house a half hour later.

Kyle met them at the door and Rick told him what they'd found.

"The fact that he didn't leave the notebook here makes me think his enemy was familiar with our home and where things were kept," Kyle noted.

"That doesn't narrow the list very much," Rick responded.

"Yeah, I hear you. Let's see if Paul and Daniel can break the code, but I have to tell you, Hosteen Silver meant for *you* to find it, so it stands to reason you hold the key," Kyle said. "You two had a special connection."

"That's because I could read people, just like Hosteen Silver did."

"I understand you kept in touch with him even when you were undercover, south of the border."

"It was only a sporadic note that would appear on a website set up by Daniel. Hosteen Silver would let me know when I had a new niece or nephew, or tell me he'd done a special Sing for my protection. Stuff like that."

"I suppose the notes were in code?"

"Yeah. He would give it to Daniel to encrypt and I had the software needed on my end to decrypt."

"Do you think he used a variant of the same system in the notebook?"

"Not likely. He didn't like computers, but it is possible it's based on a number-letter substitution with a specific book as the key. If I'm right, finding that particular book is going to require patience and a lot of luck."

AN HOUR LATER, after a quick breakfast with Kyle and Erin, Kim and Rick were in the SUV heading back to Hartley. "I remember when your foster father came to visit Uncle Frank," Kim said. "All eyes in the tavern would automatically turn to him. His white headband and of course his long silver hair made him stand out even in a crowd."

"That's why he was known as Hosteen Silver. *Hosteen* means Mister, I'm sure you know that already, having worked with Angelina. And Silver… well, that was obvious. His hair seemed to glow with a silver sheen that's impossible to describe."

"I agree. One time I was stressed out, hurrying

to finish cleaning the tables so I could get to class. He came over and told me that I already had my place in the pattern of life. I didn't have to rush to make it so."

"That sounds like him."

"I wasn't sure what he was talking about, but I didn't have time to ask," she said. "The next day when I went to work, Uncle Frank said that he'd left a note for me. I read it but it made no sense."

"What did the note say?"

"It had a tiny hand-drawn figure of a horse, and a note saying that the horse had a lot to teach me." She held up her hands, palms up and shrugged. "No explanation, nothing. Just that."

He smiled. "He was telling you that Horse is your spiritual sister."

"Why a horse? I love them, but I've never even ridden one."

"As far as he was concerned, what Eagle is to me, Horse is to you."

"Does the horse symbolize strength?" she asked, taking a guess.

"Yes, and cooperation, too. Horse is all about knowing when to exert control and when to yield. It's a reminder that you get better results when you don't try to do everything by yourself."

"I wish he would have just said that."

Rick laughed. "That wasn't his way. He liked letting things unfold in your own thinking."

After a while, her thoughts still on the case, she glanced over at him. "Do you still want to stop by Angelina's second store? Jeri, the manager, worked at Silver Heritage before her promotion and she might remember the professor's name."

"What makes you think she'd remember?"

"She thought he was hot."

"You didn't?"

She took a deep breath. "What attracts me to a man isn't looks. It's attitude. Like confidence. Integrity is essential, and courage works, too."

"Are you telling me that you're never swayed by packaging?" he said, giving her an incredulous grin.

"Hey, I like eye candy as much as the next person, but keeping my interest takes a lot more than that," she said, laughing. "I'm picky. When I met you for the first time since high school, what got my attention was the way you looked at whoever was speaking to you. That person had your undivided attention. You also took time to savor your food; you didn't just wolf it down. I knew that you were a man who took his time to do things right." Realizing the double entendre, she glanced away and felt her cheeks burning.

"I don't like to rush," he said, his voice low and deep. "Like wine, women and investigations, some things just need that extra attention."

The masculine timbre of his voice felt like a

warm caress on a cold winter's night. Realizing the turn her thoughts had taken, Kim forced herself to look directly ahead.

As she peered off into the distance, something on the road caught her attention. "Slow down. There's some kind of animal in our way." She squinted, then quickly added, "It's a snake."

"Pretty common sight this late in the year. They sometimes sun themselves in the morning just to get warm. Let me see if I can prod it off the road." He braked and came to a stop.

"Why don't you just drive around it? If it's a rattler you'll be safer keeping your distance."

"The road isn't wide enough. And if I try to straddle it, it might just move and get struck. Wait here," he said, climbing out. "I don't want to kill it unless I have to."

She watched him approach the snake, then stop and glance all around. Maybe it was already dead.

She watched him use the tip of his boot to prod it, but to her surprise, part of the snake suddenly disappeared. That's when she realized it wasn't real. She got out of the SUV and walked over. "What is it?"

"It's a fake, constructed out of colored sawdust, ash and charcoal. The pattern and materials remind me of the dry paintings Navajo witches use."

"Skinwalkers?"

He glared at her. "Don't say that word. Not

here." Looking around, he added, "Get back in the SUV. Hurry."

She heard the urgency in his voice and moved quickly. Before they were halfway there, the sharp blast of gunfire echoed against the canyon walls behind them and two holes appeared in the windshield.

"Ambush!" Rick said, grabbing Kim's arm and pulling her to the driver's side. "Get down!"

Chapter Nine

"Crawl underneath the SUV," Rick yelled as more bullets kicked up dust inches from his head.

As soon as she was beneath cover, he rolled in and lay next to her.

"We're trapped!" she said, her voice shaky.

"For now we're out of his line of sight with a lot of heavy engine metal between him and us," Rick said, reassuring her by putting his hand on her shoulder. "But we can't afford to stay pinned down under here. If we're unable to move, that'll give him time to change positions and maybe get a clear shot."

"We need to call for help."

"That's the plan." Rick rolled onto his side, brought out his phone and handed it to her. "Tell Kyle we're about a hundred yards from the highway and that the shooter is on high ground to the northwest, a couple hundred yards away from us at the moment."

"What are you going to do?"

"I'll put myself in a position to return fire and keep him from flanking us. Best case scenario, I'll pin him down or force him to move. Then we might be able to climb back inside the truck and get away."

"Okay, but be careful, please!"

"I'll be fine," Rick said, crawling prone to the passenger's side then inching out. Scrambling to his knees, he moved to the rear of the SUV and took a quick look around.

Hearing a boom and a thud as a bullet struck the rear bumper about a foot away, he ducked back.

"You okay?" Kim called out, fear alive in her voice.

"Yeah. Make the call."

"I'm waiting… Okay, he's answering," Kim told him.

Rick brought out his pistol, slipped off the safety and considered his next move. The glare off the vehicle should interfere with the shooter's sight. He moved toward the front passenger door and rose up for a look.

He watched carefully for movement and finally saw the shooter's exact location. If only he had a rifle with a scope. A direct hit with a pistol at this range would be unlikely, but he might be able to either discourage movement or, better yet, force it.

Another shot rang out. This time the bullet struck somewhere up front.

Rick looked to his left, then his right. There was no cover to speak of. If they decided to make a break for the canyon they'd get shot in the back.

"Kyle called the tribal police, but it'll take at least a half hour or more for them to arrive," Kim called out to him. "Kyle's circling around, coming from the northeast. He says he'll be within range in fifteen minutes or less."

"Okay. Just stay where you are."

"How's Kyle coming around from the east? I thought there was only one way in or out of Copper Canyon, the trail that's right behind us."

"There's another way, providing you travel on foot. Only my family knows it, though."

"So what do we do now, wait?"

Rick kept his eyes on the shooter's location and saw movement. Someone was standing. "Hang on a second."

He moved to the hood, stood and fired two shots at the sniper. Though he missed, the bullets got the shooter's attention and he dropped to the ground instantly.

A few seconds later the shooter fired again, one bullet high, the second striking the SUV in the side, passing through and whining down the road.

"That was close," Kim called out. "You okay?"

"Yeah, but he'll have to think twice about trying to work his way around us now," Rick said, looking back at the exit hole in the passenger door.

That ruled out any attempt to get behind the wheel. "Come on out, Kim, I want you behind the engine block."

He bent and looked into her dusty face. Her expression was grim but calm.

"How do we fight back?" she asked.

"We survive. Backup's on the way. Till then we have to stay alive and protect ourselves from being outflanked." He reached down and lifted her up to a crouching position. "Keep your head down."

After the longest five minutes in history, Rick's phone rang.

"He's gone." Kyle's voice was clear. "There's a truck in the distance, about a quarter mile down the highway and picking up speed. I'll call the tribal cops to see if they can set up a roadblock."

"You sure that's him?"

"Pretty sure. There's nobody on that hill anymore. All I can see through my rifle scope is a depression in the sand where the guy was lying."

Rick motioned for Kim to stay down, then looked out through the windows toward the north. There was Kyle, about a hundred and fifty yards away. Rick glanced to the south, then swept the area all around them, including back toward the canyon. Nobody was in sight.

"It's okay, Kim," he said, reaching over and taking her hand. She stood and he brought his arm around her, pulling her close. "We made it."

AFTER THE TRIBAL officers arrived, they went over to the three-dimensional charcoal-and-ash snake left for them on the road. "This was meant to get your attention, a setup to make you stop and present an easy target," Officer Begay said, taking a photo of it. "It's not really Navajo witchcraft. All the elements don't fit. Scattering ashes about in the daytime is insulting to Sun, but that's not scattered."

"So we may be talking about someone with limited knowledge of Navajo ways," Rick added.

"An Anglo maybe?" the other tribal cop, named Henderson, suggested. "Certainly something to consider." Both officers looked at Kim.

"Might be someone who works with members of the tribe who aren't Traditionalists," she replied.

"I agree," Rick said. "How about we check out the sniper's position?"

They climbed the low hill to join Kyle, who'd remained near that spot.

Officer Henderson crouched down and studied the ground. "He ignored the impression his body left in the sand, but rubbed out his footprints before he left," he said. "He wasn't trying to erase his shooting position, but he was determined to prevent us from finding a boot or shoe print to identify. No shell casings, either, or cigarette butts or hard evidence of any kind. At least we'll be able to identify the tread patterns from the pickup tires. We photographed them beside the highway."

"There are reports that you've had other problems recently," Begay said, looking at Rick. "If we go from the assumption that the two incidents are related, then you must have been the target today."

"Or perhaps your companion," Henderson said, looking at Kim. "You were at the restaurant, too, correct?"

Kim nodded. "Anyone out to hurt me could have done that weeks ago. This began after Rick returned home."

"My gut says she's right," Rick said, then told them about the falling wall. "The perp failed to take us all out at once, so now maybe he's decided to come for us one a time." He looked at Kyle and added, "Stay on your guard, just in case that's it."

RICK AND KIM signed statements that were included in the tribal police report while Kyle caught a ride back to the ranch with Erin, who'd driven up once her husband declared it to be safe. After checking to make sure the SUV was still functional, Rick and Kim were on their way to Hartley.

"I'm thinking all this has something to do with Hosteen Silver and you," Kim said, "but I'm not sure what the connection is."

He pushed the cell phone over to her. "Call

Daniel and send him copies of the notebook pages I photographed."

A moment later Daniel called back. Rick put him on the speaker, which was clearer than the cell phone.

"I'll put this through a decryption program, but I don't think we'll get far," Daniel said. "It's not the same code you and our father used earlier. You probably noticed that already."

Paul was also on the line. "I think we need to talk to Gene. He was the last one to speak to our foster father before he went missing. Hosteen Silver had asked him to go pick up the horse and board it for a while. Maybe he'll remember something useful."

"Gene's up at his ranch?" Rick asked.

"No, he's staying here at the compound," Daniel said. "And here he is now."

Gene's voice came through next. "After Preston told me what was going on, I decided to put some distance between me and my family. If someone wants to off me, I'm not running, but I want my family out of the line of fire. Some of Daniel's men are taking care of things at the ranch in case I'm on somebody's target list. In the meantime I made sure I was seen in Hartley."

"Good plan," Rick said, giving him the highlights of their conversation before he joined in.

"So what can you tell me about the last time you spoke with Hosteen Silver?"

"There was no grand revelation. He said he seldom went riding anymore and asked if I could use another ranch horse. Later that day, I went to pick up the gelding, but Hosteen Silver wasn't around. I went inside to check on things and that's when I realized something was off."

"Considering he left his private journal, the letters and the keys to his truck right there on the table, I'd say he planned things carefully. He knew he was going for his final walk," Daniel said. "Did he say anything about a code when you spoke to him?"

"No, not a thing. Just about his horse," Gene replied. "Preston came over soon after that and we searched the entire canyon, but there was no sign of him."

"He didn't want to be found," Rick said.

"By the way, Preston heard from the fire marshal. He claims that the explosion at the Brickhouse was triggered when a small piece of wood placed on the heating element of an electric hot plate produced a flame," Daniel reported.

"A very simple setup that would have probably escaped detection if the fire hadn't been put out so quickly. That establishes arson for sure," Rick replied.

"Time for a war council," Daniel said. "Are you on your way to town, Rick?"

"Yeah. I have one stop to make, then I'll head over to your compound," he answered.

"Good. We need to come up with a viable tactical plan."

After he ended the call, Kim looked at him. "Turquoise Dreams—is that where we're going?"

"Yes, I want to see if your friend remembers the professor's name and if she can give us some useful insights."

As they approached the business, they made sure Angelina's pickup wasn't there before parking.

The store was smaller than Silver Heritage, but catered to a more affluent clientele. A guard sat on a bar stool near the door and nodded to them as they came in through the small glass foyer.

Jeri ran around the counter to give Kim a hug. "I heard what Angelina did to you, and I'm so sorry! I wish I could talk her out of it, but you know how she is."

"It's okay, Jeri. I've landed an even better job." She gestured to Rick. "Have you met my new supervisor?"

Jeri smiled widely and held out her hand, offering to shake. "I'm Jeri Murphy."

"Rick Cloud," he answered, shaking her hand.

He was no Traditionalist and had no problem shaking hands with a stranger.

"So what brings you here?"

"We're trying to find someone—the young professor who came looking for Hosteen Silver," Kim said. "Do you remember him?"

"Oh, yeah. Those blue eyes…" She sighed. "What's to forget?"

"Do you recall his name, or what he teaches? All I remember is that he said he was from Durango," Kim said.

"He teaches at Fort Lewis College, and introduced himself as Tim McCullough," she said. "Why are you interested in him?"

"We wanted to know why he was interested in Rick's foster dad," she said. "If you hear anything, or if he shows up here again, let me know?"

"Sure," Jeri said. "If you find him first, tell him we carry high-quality, hand-carved fetishes here at this shop. Maybe he'll stop by. It sure would be nice to see him again. He's easy on the eyes."

Kim smiled. "I'll remember."

They started to leave the store when Rick stopped by the security guard, took a closer look at the man's face and smiled. "Big Joe! I haven't seen you since high school. I always thought you'd be playing football with the pros someday."

"Me, too, Rick, till I got injured and sat out my senior year."

"Now you're here in the security business," Rick said.

"Who'd have thought it, huh?" Joe said, laughing. Then he turned serious. "I've got friends in the P.D. who've kept me current on the situation with you and your family. Anything I can do, just say the word. When I came back from Afghanistan, Hosteen Silver helped me get my head together by doing a pollen blessing over me. I got my life straightened out again 'cause of him, so if his sons need me, I'm there."

"I never saw you as a Traditionalist, or a new Traditionalist, either," Rick said, surprised.

"The older you get, the more the Navajo Way makes sense," he said, referring to the path traditional members of the tribe followed. "It's in our blood, brother."

"I hear you. I still carry the medicine pouch my foster father gave me," Rick told him.

"Your old man definitely had what we call *'álí·l*."

Rick nodded and then, glancing at Kim, explained. "It means supernatural power, something that goes beyond what we can explain rationally."

"That's why he made enemies," Joe added. "People continually came to him wanting to become his apprentice. They all wanted to do the things he could, but he turned almost everyone away.

Remember Nestor Sandoval? The little guy in our chemistry class who never said much to anyone?"

"What about him?"

"Nestor began to walk the path of a Traditionalist and wanted your foster dad to take him on as an apprentice. After about a week, they had some kind of falling-out."

"Any idea what happened?" Rick asked.

"Hosteen Silver took his work very seriously, and in my opinion, he figured out that Nestor wanted to manipulate people, not help them."

"Interesting. What's Sandoval doing these days?" Rick asked.

"He's mixed up with a gang of Rez thugs, and let me tell you, he hates your family, especially your foster dad. To hear Nestor talk, Hosteen Silver prevented him from following The Way."

"Good to know, thanks. Any idea where I can find him?" Rick asked.

"His crew sometimes hangs out at the Taco Emporium on East Broadway. It's next door to Augustino's Pawn Shop, where they do business."

"Sandoval sounds like a good suspect," Kim said as soon as they left the store.

"I'll have my brothers run him through the system. If he has a record, we'll get a better idea of who we're dealing with."

After he made the call, Kim shifted in her seat,

facing him. "I never imagined that a medicine man would make deadly enemies."

"It's not unusual. Sings gone wrong.... Jealousy.... Hosteen Silver had a strong personality and high standards."

They were soon traveling down Hartley's main street. "I was really surprised to see Joe. I always liked him, and from what I can tell he hasn't changed much, despite all he's probably been through. I don't think he ever noticed the scar on my face. To him, I'm still just Rick."

"That's because of *you,* Rick. When you walk into a room, you own it. That's why I can't picture you working undercover anywhere. You stand out, and it's not the scar on your face."

"Is that a compliment?" he asked, enjoying the stirring he saw in her eyes and the flash of heat that coursed through him.

"It's a fact...and a compliment," she added with a tiny smile. "So how did you ever make it undercover? You just don't blend in."

He laughed. "Going undercover is tricky. You have to play a role, much like an actor, and create a whole new personality. Sometimes you do it so well, you start to forget who you really are. That's when it's time to get out," he said, his voice somber. "The fight that left me with the scar you see on my face gave me the final push I needed to come home."

"What happened?" she asked.

"That's for another time."

He'd kept his eye on the rearview mirror as he drove through Hartley. "We're being followed," he said at last.

Chapter Ten

Rick's hands tensed as he gripped the steering wheel, trying not to make any sudden moves. Patience was required until he came up with a strategy.

A few blocks farther down the street, Rick checked the mirror again. "He's staying well back, but he's still there."

Kim was about to turn around in her seat when he reached over and touched her on the shoulder. "Don't look. Glance in the side mirror, but don't do anything that'll attract his attention and signal that we've spotted him," he said. "I want to see if I can draw him out."

Rick took a slower route and paced himself to catch every stoplight. The beat-up '60s Ford pickup followed his lead and remained at least three to four car lengths behind.

"I could call my brothers and see if we can trap him between us, but he's being too careful. He'll take off the moment he smells a trap."

"When did you first notice him?"

"A few minutes after we left Turquoise Dreams." Rick slowed and turned the corner. "He's not there anymore. I think something spooked him."

Rick continued moving slowly for several more minutes, giving the tail a chance to catch up, but the truck had disappeared. They rode in silence for a while longer, then he heard a faint electronic click coming from somewhere up front.

He looked around, trying to find out what might be making the sound. Nothing was on at the moment except for the engine—not the radio, heater or anything else. "Did you just hear something?"

"That click? I thought maybe you'd switched on the cruise control or something like that," she replied.

He glanced below the instrument panel in the area of the steering column. The low tone was coming from beneath the floorboards; a hum he'd never heard before.

"I have a bad feeling about this." He pulled into the lot of an empty store with a For Rent or Lease sign in the window. "Something's wrong. Get out and get away from the vehicle."

"What is it?" she replied, throwing the door open and jumping out quickly. "Aren't you coming? What's wrong?"

"I don't know, but I want to check this out. Stay clear until I'm done." Taking a flashlight from the glove compartment, he studied the steering column, then directed the beam slowly down toward the floorboard. "Nothing."

"You think it's a bomb?" she asked, her voice unsteady. "If you do, get away from there right now and call the police."

"It's not a bomb. I've never heard one that sends out a warning. That would defeat its purpose." He climbed out his side, dropped to the asphalt and aimed the flashlight underneath the vehicle. Attached to the frame just inside the left wheel well was a black vinyl box that looked like an eyeglass case.

"I found something," he said. Where it was attached to the wheel well he saw a chunk of gray metal that had been glued to the bottom of the case. "It's attached by a magnet, like one of those hidden car key things."

He put on his gloves, detached the box and then set it on the ground about ten feet from the SUV.

"Let me take a look," she said, inching closer.

"No, stay around behind the engine block until I'm sure what this is. Could be a jerry-rigged tracking device of some sort."

"You think maybe one of your brothers put it there?" she suggested.

"My brothers wouldn't have attached something that had a tone anyone in the front seat could hear. Listen."

"It's humming."

"Stand back," he said, reaching for it with a gloved hand.

Holding it away from him, he turned his head and opened the top.

It popped loudly and threw confetti into the air. Rick automatically flinched and dropped it to the ground. A moment later, realizing that there was no danger, he bent to pick it up. "Someone's messing with us," he growled.

Kim came closer and looked at the container. "Was it some kind of firecracker?"

"No, it's a party popper. Whoever did this fixed it so that when I opened the top, it pulled a hidden string, setting it off."

"I've heard of those, but never seen one."

"Back in high school I hooked one inside Kyle's locker. He opened it up one morning and *bam!* He dropped his books, jumped about three feet and ended up looking like an idiot. He caught me and there was all hell to pay later," he said with a quick half grin.

"What's the little plastic box in there?"

"Some kind of battery-powered noisemaker, like the ones you find in some stuffed animals and toys," he answered. "Reach into the glove compartment. Dan keeps evidence bags there. I want Preston to see if he can lift prints from the case or the box."

"This may be the work of the person who left the snake fang in my apartment and that fake snake on the road. If the arsonist had done this, there would have been more than confetti and a pop by now." She'd meant to sound brave, to shrug in the face of danger, but her voice broke.

"We're okay," he said in a quiet, steady voice. "Don't let him get inside your head."

Within minutes they were on their way again. Rick drove around the block slowly, checking out the immediate vicinity.

"You're hoping to spot the old truck again?" Kim asked.

"Yeah, sure, though the odds are against it," he answered.

"Considering what Big Joe told you about Nestor Sandoval, wouldn't you say that this kind of stunt fits something he'd do?"

"Back in high school, maybe, but now that he's gang connected, a brick through our windshield might be more his speed."

As they drove past the lot where they'd been parked, Kim noticed someone enter the alley behind the empty building. "Circle the block," she said quickly. "I think I just saw Mike."

He turned the corner and drove to the other end of the alley.

"Mike, are you in here?" she called after rolling down the window.

The big man came out from the recess of a doorway. He was wearing a backpack and thick camouflage jacket.

"Hungry?" Rick called out. "I think we can rustle up a cheeseburger and some fries."

Mike didn't answer, but he pointed down the street.

"Total Burger? No problem," Rick said. "Hop in. We'll give you a ride."

Mike shook his head.

"How about if we all walk there?" Kim suggested.

Mike smiled, so Rick inched forward and parked beside the curb in a legitimate parking spot.

They strolled down the sidewalk side by side in silence. Then to their surprise, Mike spoke.

"Saw a guy watching from the alley when you removed the confetti popper from beneath the SUV. He was Navajo, five ten, maybe…jeans and a red sweatshirt that said Chieftains. When you were done, he got in a pickup and drove off."

Kim's look of surprise quickly turned into a smile.

Rick recognized the name of the Shiprock high school team. "What was he driving?"

"Old truck," Mike said. "But at least there were no bullet holes in it," he said, a trace of a smile on his face for a moment.

As they reached the fast-food place, Rick walked

to the entrance and held the door open for all of them, but Mike shook his head.

"It's okay, Mike, we'll eat out here," Kim said. Looking at Rick, she reached into her purse for her wallet. "Wanna get us all something?"

"I've got it."

Rick came back moments later and placed a sack filled with food and a milk shake in front of Mike. He had another bag with burgers and fries for himself and Kim.

They all dug in quickly and after a few minutes Rick spoke. "We're both glad to help you, soldier, but we could use your help today."

Mike took another big bite out of a burger, chewed silently for a while, then swallowed, all the time avoiding Rick's gaze. "No one will believe anything I say."

As Mike continued to eat, Rick allowed the silence to stretch out.

"You're hoping I saw someone the night of the explosion. But I didn't see anything until the day after," Mike said. "When you two were inside looking around, I saw a guy pushing against one of the damaged walls."

"Did you recognize who it was?" Rick asked instantly.

"I didn't see him clearly, just his gray hoodie and sweatpants," he said.

"Could it have been Bobby Crawford?" Kim

asked, knowing Mike would have known the staff at the Brickhouse.

"Too tall for the boy."

"Was he the same height as the man you saw watching us today?" Rick asked.

"Maybe." Mike wadded up the hamburger wrapper and tossed everything in the trash. "People don't want to look at me. That makes it easier for me to keep watch. If I hear or see anything else, I'll find you."

"Mike, there are veteran organizations—" Rick began.

Mike held up a hand, interrupting him. "No thanks. I can take care of myself." With that, he walked off down the alley.

Wanting to give Mike a card with his cell phone number, Rick raced to catch up with him, but by the time he got to the end of the block, Mike was gone.

"I should have known," he said, shaking his head as he returned.

"He's like a puff of smoke, here one second, gone the next. How does a big man like him do that?" Kim asked.

"He's learned to become invisible on the streets. It's how you keep breathing." Rick stopped at the trash can and picked up the clear plastic top to the empty milk shake container. "Let's see if I can find out who he really is."

"Mike won't like that."

"I don't have to tell him I know. I just want to know who I'm dealing with."

Hearing the haunted tone in Rick's voice, she wished she could have asked him about his life, but a man like him didn't share personal information easily. First, she would have to earn his trust and respect. Yet having him see her as an equal promised to be a tough proposition, particularly since she was now his intern.

THEY WERE IN Daniel's tactical room some time later with three of Rick's brothers. Preston had accessed Sandoval's record, which was extensive, and had sent it to one of the wall monitors.

"Nestor lives on the Rez. He's out of my jurisdiction unless he commits a crime in the city and I'm in pursuit," Preston said. "I've got his file thanks to my contact in the Shiprock P.D. I'll be meeting him later today to see what else I can find out."

"You may not be able to question Sandoval, but I can," Rick said.

"Not officially, you can't. Give me time to persuade tribal detective Bidtah to go with you. That's his turf."

"I've got practically nothing on Bobby Crawford," Paul said, looking up from the big tabletop computer. "A couple of parking tickets is all."

"My uncle would have had a background check done," Kim said. "He was always careful who we hired."

"Anything on the transient, Mike?" Rick asked Preston.

"Yes. Once I had his prints, the rest was easy. His real name is Raymond Weaver. Ray made sergeant in the army, serving with the First Cavalry. A week before he was scheduled to rotate home his recon unit was ambushed. He managed to recover and evacuate the wounded in his troop, carrying them to safety one at a time. Most of the men died while being treated, but Ray saved four lives. One of those survivors, who lost a leg, later committed suicide. Sergeant Ray Weaver, the man you know as Mike, was awarded several medals. After being diagnosed with post-traumatic stress disorder, he left the service at the end of his enlistment and dropped out of sight. No credit cards, no bank accounts, and his driver's license has expired."

"He's lost until he heals from the inside out," Rick noted in a taut voice. "PTSD isn't something you can overcome without a struggle."

"You want me to have one of our officers pick him up?" Preston asked. "Maybe we can convince him—"

"No." Rick cut him short. "That's the worst

thing you can do. He can't be pushed. He has to do this his own way."

Rick remembered his days in the hospital after being pulled out of his undercover assignment. The scar on his face had been only one of many wounds. Long months of recuperating and rehab had challenged him at every turn, and during the dark days that followed, he'd battled his own demons.

"Something about you drew him out, Rick. Was it something you said?" Kim asked.

"Not so much. I think he senses that in a lot of ways we are two of a kind." He shook his head, signaling her not to ask him any more questions.

From across the room Gene spoke up. "Kim, I think your uncle Frank might still be able to add something to the arson side of the investigation. You should talk to him."

"He was released from the hospital yesterday," Preston added. "He's home."

"I'm ready to pay him a visit as soon as you are, Rick," Kim said.

"First, you two better get another ride. The one you're in looks a little too conspicuous," Preston joked.

"Good idea." Rick grabbed a set of keys to one of Daniel's other SUVs from a hook on the wall.

"Let's go, but stay focused on Sandoval, Preston. He's involved in this and I want to know how," Rick added.

"On it," Preston answered. "I'm also going to take a real close look at Angelina Curley. For all we know, the person who clocked Frank Nelson was a woman."

"Did any of you look into Frank's silent partner, Arthur Johnson?" Rick asked.

Preston nodded. "He's a former lieutenant colonel in the marines, honorable discharge, has no record other than an old speeding ticket and drives a 2001 green Mercedes with a vanity plate that says *Ellie*. That was his wife's name. She died about eighteen months ago."

As Rick drove out of the compound in the new SUV, Kim leaned back in her seat. "I don't know much about Art, but Uncle Frank doesn't make friends easily, and he trusts him completely. That should count for something. Do you want me to ask Uncle Frank about him?"

"Sure, but don't dive right in. Ease into it."

"Do you think my uncle's hiding something?" she asked, curious about his suggestion.

"Not necessarily, but I've learned that people speak more freely and tend to remember important details when they don't feel pressured."

They were driving past what remained of the Brickhouse when Kim noticed three muscular teenage boys circling Mike, feigning punches and grabbing at his backpack. One was waving around a small baseball bat like a club.

"Those punks are taunting Mike. Ray, I mean," she said, pointing. "He needs our help."

Chapter Eleven

Rick slammed on the brakes and pulled over to the curb, but before he'd even come to a stop, Ray Weaver had taken away the bat from the first teen, flipped the second over onto a pile of plastic trash bags and was facing off with the third. The tall kid with peach fuzz sideburns tried to land a knockout punch, but Ray blocked the move easily. The kid, realizing he was out of his league, spun around and raced on the tail of his fleeing companions.

"Guess you don't need anyone covering your six," Rick said, using the military expression for watching your back.

Ray shrugged. "Not with those sorry punks. They just need to learn a little respect for their elders, but thanks for stepping up."

"No prob. They won't be bothering you again, that's for sure." Rick reached for his wallet and gave Ray a card with his telephone number. "When you're ready, Sergeant, call me. I can help you land a job and find a warm place to crash."

"You know who I am." His eyes met Rick's and something clicked. "My fingerprints were on that plastic lid you pulled from the trash."

Rick didn't answer directly. "As I said, Ray, when you're ready."

On their way again, Kim gave Rick directions to Frank's home, then opened up to him. "I experienced combat when our supply convoys came under attack. Whenever we hit the road, my nerves were always on edge, waiting to see if our vehicle was going to take an RPG strike or run over an IED. That uncertainty and fear really gets under your skin. Even after I came home, I was always looking around, gauging the threat environment. It took me a long time to become a civilian again," she said. "Is that what you think happened to Ray?"

"To a degree, yes. Right now he's trying to make his peace between who he was as a soldier and who he's supposed to be stateside," he said. "He needs to withdraw from the world to find himself again."

"You went through something like that when you left undercover work, didn't you?" she asked softly.

He nodded. "After my last assignment, I spent a lot of time in a hospital recovering from three bullet wounds and the cut you see on my face. The pain was a daily reminder of how close to death I'd come. Once the doctors had done all they could and we reached the cosmetic surgery stage, I'd had enough. I said no more and walked away. I rented a cabin up in the San Juan Mountains and stayed there for ten months. I didn't shave. I bathed in a creek. And didn't speak to anyone," he said, his voice distant. "Time—and that daily silence—mapped my way back."

"My healing came little by little on campus. A group of us would get together after class and relax by talking about inconsequential things like a new purse, or shoes, or the latest coffee flavor at Fresh Cup. Slowly I became me again."

"Finding your way back can take you down many roads, but in the end all that matters is that you made it."

As they arrived at Frank's home, Kim sat up and looked directly ahead. "The Silverado is Uncle Frank's pickup. I don't know who owns the white Toyota."

Rick got some immediate feedback from Preston, who ran the plates as they parked. "It belongs to Arthur Johnson," Rick said, viewing his phone as they walked up the sidewalk. "Looks like we got lucky."

They entered the house and Frank ushered them into the living room. Although he got around slowly, he seemed on the mend.

"I'm so glad to see you up and about, Uncle Frank," Kim said.

"Me, too. Hospitals scare me spitless," he admitted with a wry grin. "Your dad would tease me unmercifully about that," he said and laughed. "It's a good thing I was unconscious when they brought me in."

Frank looked at Rick. "Have you found any answers yet?"

"Not definitive ones, no, but we'd like to ask you a few more questions," Rick said. He could hear someone in the kitchen—no doubt Arthur—but avoided glancing in that direction, not wanting to distract Kim's uncle.

Frank gave his niece a hard look. "You convinced Mr. Cloud to let you help investigate the blast, didn't you? I know you're taking law-enforcement classes, Kim, and that you learned a lot from your dad, but you're still not a police officer."

"This is all part of my new job, Uncle Frank. I've accepted a paid internship with Level One Security, and Rick's giving me on-the-job training. It's an opportunity I couldn't pass up."

Frank's gaze hardened and he looked directly at Rick. "This is also his chance to keep you close and figure out if you know anything about who might have done this."

"I can protect her," Rick said.

"Looks to me like you haven't had much luck protecting yourself in the past," he said, his meaning clear.

"The fact that I'm standing here now proves I can handle myself."

"Good point. So how can I help you?"

"Have you given any more thought to the events leading up to the explosion?" Rick asked.

"I've thought of nothing else," Frank admitted, touching the large bandage above his right ear.

"Now that you've had a chance to look back, were there any red flags you somehow missed?"

Frank nodded. "When I went to take out some trash I heard someone in the alley behind the Brickhouse. I saw the back of someone in a hoodie walking down the alley, but I just assumed it was the homeless vet Kim feeds every night."

"How'd you know he's a vet?" Rick asked.

"He has a tattoo I recognized—some cavalry unit—and he carries himself like a soldier. I served and I recognize that walk."

"The hoodie person—you know it was a man, not a woman?" Kim asked.

"Strode like a man. Didn't have hips, either. I guess I should have taken a closer look, but I was watching the Dallas game while cleaning up."

"Do you keep the kitchen doors locked?" Rick asked.

"Not when we're open. Someone's constantly going outside to throw out trash or to take a break. We've never had any trouble before."

A moment later a man came into the room holding a mug of steaming coffee. He stood around six foot one and had silver, close-cropped hair, the perfect image of a no-nonsense former military officer.

Frank stood to introduce them. "This is my partner and friend, Arthur Johnson."

"Call me Art," he said, extending his hand and shaking Rick's. Art sized up Rick at a gaze. "I imagine your family has run a background check on me by now. What can I add to what you already know?"

Something told Rick that Art was a man who'd prefer the direct approach. "Where were you two nights ago at approximately 9:00 p.m.?" he asked, not wasting any time.

"Right to the point. I like that," Art said with an approving nod. "I was on the first leg of a flight back here from Oregon. I had a layover in Phoenix, and I didn't arrive in Hartley until around noon yesterday. If you're looking to me, or Frank, for a motive, you're wasting your time." He took a long sip of coffee from the mug.

"I understand the insurance settlement will be substantial," Rick said, though in truth he didn't have any details yet. Preston needed a court order, and going through the red tape always took time.

"I always make sure I can recoup my losses should something happen to one of my investments," Art said. "That's just good business. As it stands, though, even if the structure and contents of the Brickhouse are replaced quickly, Frank and I will still face a substantial loss of revenue during the rebuilding process."

"Is it true you aren't involved in day-to-day business at the tavern?" Rick asked.

"Never have been. I was a silent partner, and Frank made all the operating decisions. After my wife passed away, I liquidated most of my investments, but held on to the Brickhouse mostly because it always ran in the black."

"So you plan to rebuild?" Rick asked.

Art set the coffee mug down. "Frank and I haven't had time to discuss that yet. First, I want to see for myself just how big a hit the building took. Would you like to come with me? I'm going over there now."

Rick shook his head. "I've already seen what I need there."

"Then I'll say goodbye," Art concluded. "I hope you catch the weasel who jumped my partner and burned down our place."

Frank gazed out the window as Art drove away. "He's a good friend. I know he sounds cold, but Art always steps up whenever he's needed."

Rick glanced at Kim. "I need to call my brother, so I'm going to step out onto the patio and give you two a chance to catch up in private."

Rick walked out the French doors onto the

flagstone patio to call Paul. He needed someone willing to cut a few corners.

"Run a careful check on Arthur Johnson's finances," Rick told him. "Look beneath the surface."

"Am I searching for anything in particular?"

"For starters, tell me if he's in debt. He mentioned selling most of his assets, and that backs up what Kim has already told us. But we don't know his current financial situation. I'd like to know if there's any reason other than personal considerations."

"Will do. Hang on and I'll do a credit check." Paul put him on hold but quickly came back on the line. "He's got a lot of outstanding medical bills, mostly alternative treatments his health insurance refused to cover. The payments are high, but he's never late."

"That doesn't necessarily mean he's not about to go broke. Check into his bank accounts and get back to me," Rick answered.

Ending the call, Rick entered the living room just in time to catch the tail end of an argument.

"You're getting sidetracked by taking on what could be a low-paying, full-time job, Kim. Nothing's more important than your education. That's your ticket up," Frank said.

"I'll benefit from this work almost as much as I do my classes, and I won't have to work two jobs just to make ends meet. I'm staying on course, and at the end of the road, I'll be wearing a badge," she said in a quiet but firm voice.

They lapsed into silence the moment they saw Rick standing there. "You ready to go?" Kim asked Rick, her face slightly flushed.

"Sure," he said.

As they walked back to the SUV parked across the street, he asked the question foremost on his mind. "Are you having second thoughts about taking an active part in the investigation?"

"None," she said flatly. "Karl Edmonds, who teaches my Police Procedure class, called me while you were outside and Uncle Frank heard me talking to him. Edmonds doesn't think Daniel's company is a good environment for a future law-enforcement officer. He wants to talk to me at school."

"I know Edmonds doesn't like me, but there might be some bad blood between Karl and Daniel, too. Any idea why?" Rick asked.

"I don't know for sure, but there's always been friction between the police department and private investigative firms in our area—everything from salaries and rivalries to conflicting interests."

"Let's go over to the campus and we'll both talk to Edmonds."

"Sounds good to me," she said, liking the way he'd offered to stand with her on this. Rick was a rock in times of trouble. His mixture of testosterone and gallantry was one she couldn't resist.

Once they arrived on campus, they headed directly for Karl's office, actually a cubicle among a dozen others in a large metal portable building. Except for Edmonds, the building was empty at the moment.

Edmonds smiled at Kim when she knocked on the doorless partition, but once he noticed Rick standing beside her, he scowled. "I'd like to talk to Miss Nelson privately, if you don't mind, Mr. Cloud." His wording was polite, his tone not even close.

"It's okay with me if Mr. Cloud remains, Mr. Edmonds," Kim answered without emotion.

Edmonds kept his eyes on Kim as he ushered them to seats. "I wanted to speak with you about your work at Complete Security. I don't know if you're aware that private investigation agencies in our area are known for cutting corners. They walk a thin line between legal and illegal practices, and that's going to hurt your chances of getting into the police academy."

Rick replied before Kim could speak. "Level One Security is led by a highly trained former military intelligence officer with a higher clearance level than anyone currently serving with your department.

"The company also works under contract for

state and federal agencies. Local public law enforcement often enlists their services for special investigations."

Karl shrugged, ignoring Rick's remarks. "You're free to make your own decisions, Kim, but the way security firms conduct their business is a lot different from the way the police department works. You're headed in the wrong direction, no matter what Rick's telling you."

Rick leaned closer. "Exactly what am I telling her, Karl?"

Edmond's gaze locked with Rick's. "You're placing this woman in danger she's not trained to face. Your entire family has enemies here, Cloud, and Kim isn't ready for the truckload of trouble you and your brothers can bring her way."

"I'm already involved, Mr. Edmonds," Kim said. "Someone tried to kill me two days ago, and I'm not going to sit back and let them have another go at me."

"That's another reason you shouldn't be involved. You're too close to it. Cops aren't allowed to investigate cases they're personally involved in." Edmonds stopped, then gave Rick a stony glare. "Or are you using her as bait?"

Rick moved forward but Kim grabbed his arm. "Come on. We're leaving."

Once they were on the sidewalk, Kim shook her head angrily. "What's gotten into him? He was sure doing his best to provoke you into taking a swing. No way that was all about me."

"Let me call Daniel to find out the history between them."

As they walked to the parking lot, Rick made a quick call. A few minutes later he had his answer.

"Before Karl got the job with the bomb squad, he'd applied for a job at Daniel's company. Something about him rubbed Daniel wrong, so he ended up hiring someone else."

"What exactly was the problem?" Kim asked.

"Daniel wouldn't say," Rick answered, "but he wants Preston to know what went down today."

"Do you think Karl Edmonds might have had something to do with the explosion? He was angry at Daniel and you, so maybe after three or four years of stewing on it, he decided to take action."

"As far as theories go, that's not so far-fetched. This was the first time Daniel and I have been together in years, at least in a place that was vulnerable to attack."

"And Edmonds does know how to blow things up," Kim said.

"Still, I'm not ready to put him on my short list—not without a stronger motive," Rick said. "Right now I've got another idea I want to check out."

Chapter Twelve

"We need to think outside the box on this," Rick said as they drove away from the campus. "My gut's telling me that you and the rest of the staff at the Brickhouse were just in the wrong place at the wrong time. My family seems to be the focus of the attack, and somehow I think it ties back to Hosteen Silver."

Kim watched him. He looked so relaxed behind the wheel, but his gaze was restless, taking in everything around them. That intensity was part of what drew her to him. He was a man who lived on the edge, one who'd dealt with brutality and conquered it, but had yet to open his heart to gentleness. She wanted to be there for him, to soothe all those rough edges, yet it was difficult penetrating the steel walls he'd built around himself.

Annoyed with herself because she'd allowed her thoughts to wander, she focused back on business. "Even if we accept that there's someone out to kill all your family, why did he wait till now? What's changed?"

"Good question. My gut tells me that once we get an answer to that, the case will crack wide-open," he said, giving her a quick smile.

His entire expression softened when he gave her one of his rare smiles. Despite what he thought, the scar didn't diminish his looks. It added to that earthy quality he possessed, and made him even more appealing.

"What are you thinking about?" he asked, his eyes dancing as if he'd already guessed.

Flustered, she thought fast. She couldn't admit to fantasizing about his looks. "I'm sure some of the answers we're searching for will come to us after you crack the code your foster dad left you."

"Good point. Let's go pay Daniel a visit to see if they've made any progress on that front."

When they arrived at the compound they joined Daniel and Paul in the main room. Rick immediately asked them about the code.

"We've run every decryption program we have and we've still got nothing," Daniel said.

"If you ask me, you're both going too high-tech on this," Paul said, looking at Rick. "The old man thought you could figure things out without a mainframe computer, so the key has got to be something you two did together or spoke about."

"A lot of time has gone by since he and I spoke at any length, but we never really talked about private stuff beyond day-to-day decisions. Even as a kid I avoided the touchy-feely stuff, and he never pushed it."

"Yet he left the book with the code in a place where only you'd be likely to find it," Daniel insisted.

After a long thoughtful pause, Daniel continued. "I have an idea. Kyle and Erin will be gone from Copper Canyon for a day or two. They're meeting potential clients in Albuquerque, so you'll have complete run of the place. Relax, look around, and maybe something will come to you. The key is, don't force it."

"I agree with Daniel," Paul said. "We'll concentrate on finding and interviewing Professor McCullough, and you work on trying to find any possible link between what happened to Hosteen Silver and the explosion at the Brickhouse."

"Okay, but there's someone I want to meet face-to-face first. What do you have for me on Nestor Sandoval?" Rick asked Paul.

"He was picked up for drug trafficking six months ago, but the case fell apart when witnesses recanted and he walked. Sandoval's stayed under the radar since then, but the police suspect he's dealing weapons now," Paul said. "He's bad to the bone, Rick, so if you're going to go searching for him, take Detective Bidtah, like Preston suggested."

Rick considered it, then nodded. "I'll head back to the Rez. See if Preston can arrange for Bidtah to meet us at Sandoval's residence."

AFTER GETTING SANDOVAL'S ADDRESS, Rick and Kim left Daniel's compound and headed west. Rick finally asked the question that had been on his mind. "Are you okay staying at the ranch alone with me? As you pointed out once before, backup's a ways off."

"Of course."

He smiled. He'd been like her at the beginning of his career—eager to work, wanting to do the right thing and refusing to back away from danger.

"We both know there's more going on between us than business," he said in a quiet voice. "That's bound to complicate things."

She sat a little straighter. "No, it won't. I barely know you, Rick. You're not exactly an open book."

"No, I'm not," he admitted.

"From what you told your brothers about your relationship with Hosteen Silver, that's just your way."

"Maybe so," he answered, not bothering to argue the point. "Life teaches all of us different lessons—or maybe it's the same lesson and we all react differently to it."

She saw the muscles on his face tighten.

"My brothers and I were all headed in the wrong direction when Hosteen Silver found us. He helped put us back together again, though unfortunately, old wounds don't always disappear. They turn into scars, reminders that none of us is as tough as we'd like to be."

"It's hard to trust a perpetual stranger, Rick. I want to know the man who'll have my back."

"Fair enough," he said after a beat. "Ask me whatever you want."

"How did you end up in foster care?" When he didn't answer right away, she added, "Do you want me to ask you something else?"

"No, it's okay," he said, then continued. "I was born to a single mother and abandoned at a trading post when I turned six. I never saw my mother again after that. By the time Hosteen Silver found me, I'd gone through a series of foster homes. I was trouble and most families couldn't wait to get rid of me. That was fine. I'd already learned never to count on anything or anyone outside myself. He found me in family services, offered me a chance to turn my life around, and it worked out, though it wasn't easy for either of us."

He'd told her his story quickly, factually and

without emotion. He didn't want her to realize how painful his past still was.

"Before you start feeling sorry for me, you should know that I like my life," he added quickly. "My brothers and I are close and I've achieved what I set out to do when I left the Rez."

"And now?"

"I've left the Bureau, so I'm in transition again. Life will show me what's next."

"You need a new passion, something that calls to you like the work you did for the Bureau. You need to find a new dream."

"I'm not a dreamer. I'm a doer."

"The two go hand-in-hand. What would you like to see in your future—a family and kids, like your brothers?" she pressed.

"I suppose I'll marry someday, but if I do, it won't need to be out of love. That emotion can change in the blink of an eye."

"So you'll marry…out of expediency?"

"No, more out of friendship and respect. Those tend to last longer."

"I've heard of worse reasons for getting married," she said, "but I won't settle for anything less than love."

"You're a beautiful woman—independent, smart," he said. "I can't imagine you not having guys lined up at your door, wanting to take you out."

"Thanks, but the truth is I'm hard to deal with. Back in high school my friends would go for the predictable guys, the pretty boys, the bad boys or the ultramacho jocks. I wasn't into any of them."

"What type of guy do you want?"

She shrugged. "I'll know him when I see him. He'll speak to my heart and be someone who needs me as much as I'll need him."

They were on Highway 64 just east of the town of Shiprock when he saw the emergency lights of a white tribal police SUV coming up from behind. "I have a feeling that's Detective Bidtah. He knew which road I'd be on."

Rick pulled over and a moment later a plain-clothes officer approached, his badge clipped to his belt.

"Rick?" he asked. "I'm Detective Allan Bidtah. One of our undercover people found out that Sandoval was evicted from his old residence. He's moved to a new place north of Shiprock on the Cortez highway. There's a rumor that he's involved with a particularly violent gang that's been causing problems in Rez communities south of Shiprock. If that report's correct, you're going to need armed backup."

"All right. Lead the way. We'll follow you."

Ten minutes later they were heading north in the direction of Colorado. They left the highway just past Monument Rocks and entered a run-down rural area, what appeared to be the beginnings of a housing development that had fizzled out. All that remained was graveled roads and a grid of scattered single-wide mobile homes. Some stood on concrete pads laid as foundations for permanent homes, and most were surrounded by chain-link fences.

Bidtah parked on a dusty road between two single-wides, then stepped out of his vehicle. He pointed to the front end of a black Nissan sedan behind the closest trailer.

Rick nodded. "You're not armed, Kim, so you should probably stay in the vehicle," he said.

"No chance. I'm supposed to be learning from you, and I can't do that if I duck and cover."

He bit back a smile. He hadn't expected anything less. "Follow my lead, stay behind me and keep your eyes open for anything that doesn't look right."

With Bidtah, they walked over, keeping space between them, not wanting to present too easy a target.

"Sandoval, open up. Detective Bidtah, tribal police," the detective said, knocking hard on the metal door. Rick watched the corner of the trailer, making sure nobody came out the back.

Several seconds went by before there was the sound of footsteps inside. The door opened slowly and four young men in their late teens, wearing baggy pants and hooded sweatshirts, came out onto the stacked warehouse pallets that served as the step. If they were armed, no weapons were visible.

"Sandoval's not here, officer. Hasn't been around for several days, maybe a week," announced a big, barrel-chested guy with a shaved head crowned with a red bandanna.

"Where can we find him?" Bidtah demanded.

"Don't know. If you get to him first, tell him Billy's looking for him."

"That makes you Billy. How about a last name?"

"Why get all cops-and-robbers on me? I ain't done nothing," Billy said.

"Talk to me here, Billy, or at the station," Bidtah said, looking back and forth at the other three, who'd stepped off the pallets and were slowly starting to form a circle.

Rick recognized the flanking maneuver. He got set, used to being the first target because of his size. He knew what was coming.

Billy nodded slightly to the others, then rushed Rick, jabbing for his throat.

Rick sidestepped the punch, dropped his shoulder and sent the big guy flying into the air. Billy hit with a thud and Rick immediately moved in, placing his foot at the guy's throat. "Don't move."

Bidtah had his weapon out now, covering two

of the others, who had their hands out, palms up, to show they were unarmed.

Out of the corner of his eye, Rick saw the fourth young man lunge for Kim. The teen threw his forearm up around her neck in a choke hold, but Kim sagged suddenly, elbowed him in the gut and stomped on his instep with her heel. As he gasped, letting go momentarily, she turned and punched him in the groin with her fist.

In agony, he sank to his knees.

Kim stepped away, turning to face the others. "Come on, guys, now that you've stood up to the cops, let's talk. Obviously you like Sandoval even less. And guess what, we don't like him, either. If you give us a lead so we can track him down, we'll all come out ahead. Make sense?" she asked, remaining perfectly calm.

"Or we can go to the station and talk breaking and entering, assault on a police officer and civilian and whatever else I can come up with between now and then," Bidtah added. "One look at the broken latch on the trailer door tells me you didn't gain entry with a key. Whose screwdriver is that anyway?" He pointed at the tool on the ground.

"So we help you find Sandoval and we're off the hook?" Billy asked.

"There's a saying, 'my enemy's enemy is my friend,'" Kim said. "At the moment, that means we're all on the same side."

"Yeah, okay," Billy said, nodding to the others. "Sandoval burned my crew. We don't owe him anything except the big hurt. What's your game?"

Kim held his gaze and kept her cool, not looking over at Rick or Bidtah for support. She knew that the gang members would probably see that as a sign of weakness. "Sandoval's in the wind. Any idea why?"

"He's worried about some heavy hitter Navajo guys, the sons of a *hataalii* he ripped off."

"Ripped off how? Money?" Kim pressed.

"Not even. The old man had taken on a student, Angelina something, so he could teach her medicine man stuff. Anyway, when the *hataalii* found out she'd been recording his Sings and sneaking photos with her cell phone, he grabbed it from her and ran her off. Sandoval heard Angelina had been planning to sell the Sings to a local college professor writing some book, so Sandoval offered to get the phone back for maybe two hundred bucks."

"But how do the sons of the *hataalii* figure into it?" Kim asked.

"When Sandoval went looking for the cell phone, the *hataalii* caught him red-handed. Sandoval roughed him up a little and got away, but not long afterward, the *hataalii* disappeared. Now Sandoval's afraid his sons will think he offed the old man."

"You got that from him?" Rick asked.

"Yeah. I can't say for sure, but I think Sandoval's also the one who placed a bounty on one of the *hataalii*'s sons. Word reached us a few days ago that anyone who takes out the marked man is in for some serious cash." He looked at Rick and studied his face. "I'm guessing that's you."

"But you're not sure of the source?" Rick persisted.

"No, and I didn't bother to find out. We're not stepping into a gig like that. We do our own thing," Billy said.

Rick suddenly heard the sound of a car engine moving toward them at high speed. As he turned his head, he saw a plume of dust trailing behind the beat-up silver sedan racing up the dirt road. There were three people inside. Two of them on the passenger's side, front and back, were wearing baseball caps. The car made a hard right, then headed directly for them.

As the car swung around broadside to the trailer, the two passengers reached out their windows, pistols in hand.

"The Diablos," Billy yelled, diving to the dirt just as bullets started to fly.

As Detective Bidtah dropped to one knee and returned fire, Rick grabbed Kim's shoulder and pulled her to the ground.

The attack only lasted a few seconds before the sedan accelerated and disappeared into the freshly generated smoke screen of sand, dust and gravel.

Chapter Thirteen

They got up slowly, looking around to see if anyone had been hit. Rick concentrated on Kim, and as soon as he verified she was okay, turned to Bidtah. The tribal cop was on his cell phone, calling in the incident as he brushed the sand from his pants with his free hand. He seemed no worse for wear.

Rick looked over at Billy and saw pure hatred in his eyes. "Cool down, man," Rick warned.

"How do I know you didn't bring them here?"

"We were *not* followed," Rick assured him. "The detective and I know how to spot a tail. At least nobody got hit," he added, looking at the other gang members now on their feet and dusting themselves off.

"The Diablos know where we hang, bro," one of the three boys said. "After last week—"

"Drop it!" Billy ordered, turning toward the boy. "Don't be putting our business out on the street like that."

He looked back at Rick. "From me to you, dude,

you stick out—the big Navajo with the scar on his face—so watch your back. And don't worry, lady, if we see Sandoval I'll pass the word along." He turned to the detective. "You're Bidtah, right?"

Bidtah nodded and gave Billy his card. "Cell number is on the back."

After the four gang members drove away, Bidtah went to his unit. Rick noticed Kim reach up to touch her shoulder and wince.

"I thought you were okay," he said.

"I am. I just landed wrong."

"Putting something cold on it will help," Rick said, walking with her toward the SUV. "We'll get you an ice pack."

Bidtah came over and joined them. "Patrol cars are out looking for the silver sedan. I don't know if Preston mentioned it to you, but the Rez gangs have changed a lot since you and your brothers lived here. They're trying to control some parts of the Rez turf. If there's a price on your head, you're going to need to be on full alert. What they lack in training, they more than make up in brutality."

"I hear you," Rick said.

Bidtah handed him his card. "If you have a problem or need some backup don't hesitate to call me."

"Thanks for all your help," Rick said as they parted ways.

Once they reached the main highway again, he

and Kim drove west toward Copper Canyon, his gaze continually darting to the rearview mirror.

"Once we get home and take care of your shoulder, I'm going for a long, slow walk around the house and the shed. Maybe what I need to break Hosteen Silver's code is one particular memory, something I haven't thought about in years."

"Become the teenager you were back then. See things through his eyes."

Rick called Preston on the car phone to update him.

"That professor keeps coming into the picture, and it's got to be the same guy."

"Probably, but I have a hard time seeing a professor as a hit man," Preston said, his sour voice mirroring his mood, from what Rick could tell.

"McCullough's cultivated sources in the Four Corners that seem to be at the heart of this case," Rick noted. "Don't write him off yet."

After hearing that they were on the way to Copper Canyon, Preston said, "I'm not sure if that's a safe place for you anymore, particularly if you're being targeted by the gangs."

"Let them take one of their low-slung rides into the canyon. They'll either high center on sandstone or be so worn out from getting unstuck they'll turn around and head back down the highway," Rick said.

Preston laughed. "Probably so," he said, adding,

"I'm going to send you the photo I found of Professor McCullough. It was on a college social website. I don't know how old the photo is, but see if Kim can make a positive ID. I'm also sending you a copy of a paper he wrote for an anthropology journal.

"One last thing," Preston added. "I ran a background on Angelina Curley. Although her husband's death was ruled a suicide, there were some unanswered questions."

"Like what?" Rick asked.

"The man died in his garage from carbon monoxide poisoning, and there was a suicide note next to him that matched up with his desktop printer. The department spoke to friends and neighbors, but the only person who claimed he'd been acting strangely was Angelina. There was no real evidence of foul play, however, so Angelina inherited his money and the business."

"Good to know, but at the moment, Nestor Sandoval's at the top of my list," Rick said and ended the call.

Kim turned in her seat to face him. "I don't think Sandoval should be our prime suspect. Maybe he played a role, but we're dealing with a multilayered case. Until we have a lot more answers, nothing is going to fit together."

"What makes you so sure?"

"Intuition," she said.

"Intuition's good, but you have to make sure it's not just wishful thinking or your own bias. You want it be Angelina, don't you?"

"Maybe I do," she admitted grudgingly, "but unfortunately she has an alibi. She was scheduled to speak to an association of minority business-women during your welcome-home event. She'd been practicing that speech for weeks."

"Yeah, and the brief glances we've gotten of the suspect suggest it's a man."

"She could have hired out," Kim said.

"She may also have canceled her plans at the last minute," Rick said, then called Preston back. "Did you ever speak to Angelina Curley about her alibi for the night of the explosion?"

"I checked it out. She was speaking to the MWA—Minority Women in Action. People saw her there and there's a DVD of the event that shows her staying late to talk to the participants."

"Okay, thanks," Rick said, disconnecting before he told Kim what he'd learned. "She's still a viable suspect, but stop trying to make the facts fit. It's an occupational hazard, I know, but what we need is hard evidence."

THEY ARRIVED AT the house thirty minutes later. The weather had turned cold, with the jet stream bringing down much cooler air from the north.

Rick built a fire while Kim checked out the materials Preston had sent them.

"How's your arm?" he asked. "We keep reusable ice packets in the fridge. I'll get you one."

"Ice packs on a cold day. Brrrr," she said, pressing it to her shoulder when he returned.

He smiled. "Don't use it for more than twenty minutes," he said. "I remember that from my high school football injuries."

His concern washed over her like a gentle warm breeze. He was the toughest, strongest man she'd ever met, yet he could still show gentleness.

"Preston said he copied the file from your phone onto the computer over here," she said, walking to the reconverted closet where the electronics were kept.

He pulled up a chair and sat beside her in front of the computer as she opened the file folder. She could feel the warmth of his body envelope her, and that made it hard for her to think clearly.

Locating the photo that Preston had sent, she took a moment to study it and nodded. "McCullough was much younger when this photo was taken, but it's him."

They used the link in Preston's email to read Professor McCullough's paper.

"The prof refers to his primary source only by initials, but A.T. could be Angelina Tso," she said. "He also admits that there were other *hataaliis* he'd wanted to interview, since most specialize in two or three types of Sings only, but they wouldn't cooperate."

"That doesn't surprise me," Rick said. "The spoken word has power, so Sings would lose their effectiveness if everyone discussed them freely. Anglo professors interested in padding their résumés with tribal ceremonial secrets are generally avoided like the plague."

Kim sat back, thinking. "This paper is interesting, but it's far from a motive for killing anyone."

"I agree."

Rick stood and turned, looking across the main room. "We've made some progress. Now let's see if there's something else I can do. It's time for me to visualize what this place looked like when I was growing up. My brothers updated it, but the past is still here. Like those bookcases," he said, pointing across the room. "I helped Hosteen Silver build those."

"He read a lot?"

"Yes, we all did, usually together. We had a TV, but it only got local channels and we were limited to two hours a night. Our dad loved reading history books, particularly those covering the Southwest or anything dealing with the Navajo code talkers."

"They were radio operators for mostly Marine units in the Pacific theater, right?" she asked and saw him nod. "We read about them in school."

"They transmitted messages the Japanese were never able to figure out by developing a sub code using Navajo words for military terms. For example, the word for *navy* was comprised of the Navajo words for *needle, ant, victor* and *yucca*. And the code word for *tank* was the Navajo word for *turtle*."

"Do you think that's the code Hosteen Silver used?"

"No," he said. "That required those at both ends of the message to know the code, which never varied," he said. "But his interest in codes was always there. That may have led him to use one that required something simpler, like a reverse-sequence key based on identical books. Anyone reading the message would just see numbers, but those numbers might indicate the page number, line number, word number or character number within that word. For instance, a number sequence 39, 14, 25, 5 could mean you look at the fifth letter of the twenty-fifth word on the fourteenth line on page thirty-nine of the book. That letter could be an *a*."

"Okay, so each set of numbers gives you letters to spell words, and once you know the words and the sequence, you know the message," she said.

He nodded. "The reason it would be hard to break is that the letter *a* could have a different number sequence every time it appeared. No pattern. Unless you had an identical copy of the book, you couldn't decode the message."

"If you're right, figuring out which book he used is going to be tough," she said.

"There are several dozen books still on the shelves, but over time the majority of what was there has been given away, taken home by one of my brothers or lost. We may not even have the particular book Hosteen Silver used anymore." He was about to say more when his cell phone rang. Looking at the screen, he saw it was Preston.

"I did some more digging on McCullough," Preston told him. "He took a sabbatical to conduct field research and he's currently at an Anasazi dig on the Rez."

"Where?" Rick asked.

"About twenty miles southeast of the ranch house. It's on a low bluff about a quarter mile above the old riverbed. A recently formed arroyo apparently exposed some artifacts."

"I think it's time we went to talk to him," Rick said.

"Something else… I spoke to Detective Bidtah. The professor's already been warned twice about straying off the site. Once more and he loses his permit."

"Okay, good to know. If I don't find him at the dig, we'll look around."

"I'll text you the GPS coordinates for the site," Preston added.

After Rick disconnected, he glanced at Kim and filled her in. "Let's go pay him a visit."

"Excellent idea."

En route he decided to take a shortcut, using the GPS on his phone to zero in on the location. Turning off the graveled road, Rick headed across an area of sandstone bedrock and shallow depressions where pools formed during the rainy season—when there was one.

The next half mile was filled with jarring, gut-crunching drops as they bounded along the desert landscape.

"This washer-board road is more like a death wish than a shortcut," Kim said.

"We should be able to cut a few minutes of travel time this way and, coming in from another direction, we'll arrive without giving anyone much warning."

As they topped a rise he said, "There they are, just below us."

Below was a narrow arroyo leading to the river through a break in a sandy plateau that extended for miles. An angular section of hillside had been carved out of the side of the arroyo. It was about three feet deep and wide, with neat, squared corners. A man in tan-colored pants and jacket was crouched within the dug-out section, examining the strata with the help of a small, bright lantern.

Around him wooden stakes and posts were laid

out in a pattern that defined the site, which extended in a string-outlined rectangle about the size of a large house. Wooden screens with wire mesh bottoms were being loaded into the back of a white Land Rover carry-all by two college-aged men wearing green boonie hats. Beside the first vehicle was a light green Jeep.

"When you said a 'dig,' I envisioned more than three people," Kim said. "I had in mind a camp with tents or RVs, floodlights and a dozen or so student volunteers."

"This is clearly a low-budget operation," he said. "It's getting late, too, and this isn't the kind of place you want to be once the sun sets. You could easily drive off a trail and end up stuck all night."

"Good point," she said, watching as the younger men finished loading their gear and climbed into the carry-all. The vehicle started up and then headed out along two ruts that comprised a route to the site. "Now that the students are gone, looks like we'll have the professor all to ourselves, assuming he's the guy still at the excavation."

As Rick parked beside the Jeep, the man in the arroyo looked up.

Just as soon as Kim got out of the SUV, the man smiled, recognizing her. Then he took another look at Rick, turned off the lantern and walked over to meet them.

"I'm surprised to see you out here, Kim," he said. "That's your name, right?"

"Yes, Professor McCullough. I'm glad you remembered. I'm helping investigate what happened at the Brickhouse Tavern," she said.

"I heard it was a case of arson," the professor said.

"From who?" Rick asked.

"Just here and there," he answered, then focused on Rick. "Are you the son of the medicine man known as Hosteen Silver?"

"I am," Rick answered.

"Well, talk about serendipity! I've been trying to find out what happened to the *hataalii*. All anyone would tell me is that he's gone."

"We believe he walked off into the desert to die. It's the way of our Traditionalists when their time draws near."

"I know, and I'm sorry to hear that," he said. "I was hoping to work with him. I've been trying to preserve and document Navajo healing traditions. Word of mouth is uncertain because it's subject to opinions and memory, but a written record would be there for generations to come. Would you or your brothers be willing to help me?"

"Our medicine men don't allow Sings to be recorded or written down in their entirety. Sharing that kind of knowledge indiscriminately is believed to be dangerous."

McCullough's eyebrows knitted together. "You don't strike me as a Traditionalist."

"I'm not and neither are my brothers, but we respect our foster father's wishes on something like this."

"All right, I understand. How about this instead? His paraphernalia—the artifacts used for the Sings... No one will use them now because of the *chindi.* If I could buy them from you, or maybe you could donate—"

Rick held up his hand, interrupting McCullough. "We have no idea what he did with them. He clearly took care of those things before he left for his final walk." Rick paused, then added, "Tell me something, professor. Do you normally offer to pay people for information?"

"I did at the beginning. I thought it might speed things along, but it didn't," he admitted. "Angelina Tso, a former medicine woman, seemed more cooperative after I offered to pay for her time. She delivered a few of the Sings, but when she found out that I'd have to verify their accuracy with another healer, she refused to have anything further to do with me."

"You didn't trust her?" Kim asked.

"My reputation is on the line with every monograph or article I write, and having two or three independent sources is standard practice," he said.

"I was sorry to lose her, but it was the weird stuff that happened afterward that bothered me most."

"Like what?" Kim queried.

"A few weeks later someone vandalized my car and office. I was sure it was her because I found ashes scattered everywhere—a bad omen for most Navajos—but I couldn't prove she was responsible."

"You'd had problems with Angelina but you still came to her shop looking for help? How come?" Kim was curious.

"I made sure she wasn't there before I went in. I knew she had contacts, so I wanted to talk to the clerks. I'd hoped to get the names of some high-end carvers. One of the papers I'm currently researching deals with the power of fetishes and their role in the Hopi and other Southwestern tribal cultures," he said, then checked his watch.

"All right then," Rick said, sensing this was all they'd get for now. "Thanks for your time."

"If you find anything among your foster father's possessions that might shed light on what it was like to be a *hataalii* of his stature, I'd appreciate the chance to catalog it—keeping the name of the source confidential, of course. A copy of my paper will go to the Navajo community college at Tsaile, so you'd be adding to the tribe's storehouse of knowledge."

"I don't think we can help you with that, not yet anyway," Rick said.

"You want closure first," he said, nodding.

Rick didn't reply. As was customary, he didn't say goodbye, either, he simply walked back to the SUV with Kim.

"He's right about one thing," Kim observed gently. "You and your family need closure. Once you know what really happened to your foster father, the rest will fall into place."

"Let's go back to the ranch house. I need a chance to think."

Once they were on the highway again, Rick's attention focused on something on the road ahead.

"What's going on?" she asked.

"Maybe nothing. There's a pickup coming in our direction, and he's really making time. Could be kids, a drunk or just someone in a hurry. Seat belt on?"

"Always. Better give him as much road as you can," she advised. "He's not slowing down."

As she spoke, the pickup eased toward the center line of the two-lane highway.

Rick touched the brakes again and eased to the right, hugging the shoulder. Though they'd avoided a head-on, the pickup driver tossed something out his window.

Glass shattered onto the SUV's reinforced windshield and quickly coated Rick's side with a black, flowing goo that completely blocked his view.

"Hang on!" he yelled.

Chapter Fourteen

Rick held the SUV's steering wheel steady, took his foot off the gas and looked out the side window to gauge his position on the road. He already knew the big vehicle tracked well, so if he could keep it on the highway…

"Can you see anything ahead?" he asked Kim, whose side of the windshield wasn't completely covered.

"You're doing great, drifting just a little to the right. Just hold us steady," she advised.

As they slowed to a crawl, he looked over. "How close to the shoulder am I?" he asked.

"About three feet. You can come over just a little more. Gently… That's good."

He braked and came to a full stop, flipping on the emergency blinkers to warn oncoming traffic, despite not seeing any vehicles.

"You okay?" he asked, glancing over.

"I'm fine, just a little rattled. I knew something was wrong after the way he raced up to us like that, playing chicken like in the movies. For a second I thought we were dead."

"Did you catch the plates?"

"No, he went by in a flash and I was too worried about where *we* were going," she said, her voice thick with fear and adrenaline.

"I'll call Bidtah. That's paint on the windshield. You can tell by the smell."

"Maybe he can get prints from one of the pieces of glass," she suggested. "Good thing it was a glass bottle, not a big rock…or bullets."

"We're both okay and the SUV is still in working order, so let's take it as a win," Rick said.

"Some win," she muttered.

BIDTAH AND TWO crime scene techs arrived twenty minutes later. At their insistence, Rick and Kim stayed inside the SUV as they collected evidence.

"This SUV is built like a tank," Bidtah said, coming over to them. "The impact of the paint-filled jar didn't even crack the windshield."

"Were any of the pieces of glass big enough to lift a print?" Rick asked.

"No. All we know is that the container was a twenty-ounce pickle jar—still had the label attached. But we did get a partial from the lid, which escaped being coated with paint except on the inside surface."

"If possible, can you share your findings with my brother Preston?"

"I sent him what I have and will keep him updated," Bidtah said. "One more thing. I took a close look at a sample of the paint, and there's something else mixed in there. I could see the particles. They could have been small clods, I suppose, except some were porous."

"What do you think it was?" Rick asked.

"My guess is either bits of pumice or corpse powder."

"Pumice, I know about," Kim noted. "We use it to clean the grill at the Brickhouse. But corpse *what?*"

"It's said our skinwalkers dig up the bones of the dead, grind them into powder, then use that as a weapon," Bidtah told her.

"Ugh," she said with a grimace.

"There's something else you need to be aware of," Bidtah added, looking at Rick and then at Kim. "If people around here see you as cursed, or subject to being cursed, they'll avoid you. People will stop talking and you'll be ostracized," Bidtah pointed to his belt. "That's why my men and I carry a medicine pouch."

"I have one, too," Rick said, pulling it out of his pocket, "but I think it's time I fastened it to my belt and made it easier to see."

"Excellent idea," Bidtah said, then added before leaving, "You should consider carrying one, too, Kim."

She nodded. "Thanks."

Fortunately, the paint was water-based, so after wiping away the paint with paper towels and bottled water from their emergency kits, they'd managed to restore enough visibility to make it to a trading post and hose down the SUV.

"I've decided to push my brothers into helping me find our foster father's body," Rick said as they made their way back to Copper Canyon. "It's too late to follow a trail, but we know he left on foot, so together we can make some intelligent guesses concerning where he might have gone. Then we'll know, once and for all, if he died of natural causes or if he was murdered."

"Most of you have law-enforcement training. How come you never checked into this before?"

"We talked about it, but the truth is none of us was ready to accept his death. As long as there was no body, we could all hang on to the hope he'd turn up again someday. There was also the matter of accepting his wishes and respecting Traditionalist ways. We all believed, at first, that he had gone off to die."

"Do you think they'll help you look for his body now?"

"Yes, but it won't be easy for any of us." He glanced over at her. "Bidtah was right, though. If you're going to continue to take part in the investigation, you'll need a medicine pouch. First, we'll get you the fetish of a horse. You can carry it in the pouch with pollen, a symbol of well-being, and a crystal, which stands for the spoken prayer. Together they have the power to make your prayers come true."

"What a beautiful tradition."

"That it is."

SURPRISINGLY, ALL HIS brothers were in agreement with the plan to search for Hosteen Silver's body. Kyle had also abandoned his trip in favor of joining in. Those who could attend met at the ranch house at nine the next morning, accompanied by Detective Bidtah, who, as a tribal cop, had official law-enforcement jurisdiction.

The two newcomers joined Rick, Kyle and Kim at the kitchen table while Erin was out feeding the horses.

"Rick, searching for our foster father's remains is going to be very difficult," Preston said, taking a sip of freshly brewed coffee. "First of all, no one on the Navajo Nation is going to feel comfortable speaking of the dead. That means establishing his whereabouts on that last day is going to be nearly impossible."

"I agree with Detective Bowman. You're not going to get any cooperation. There isn't a crime to speak of, so most will see what you're doing as disrespecting the old ways and the *hataalii*'s wishes," Bidtah said. "If I were in your boots, I'd concentrate on the battles you have a chance of winning."

"We can still question possible witnesses, and we will," Preston said. "We just have to remain respectful and not be so direct."

"Kim and I will try to retrace the likely steps Hosteen Silver may have taken when he left here for the last time," Rick said. "I recall that he liked to go to the Totah Café in the mornings. It's an hour's walk from here, a short distance by Navajo standards. There's always a chance that he might have gone there the day of his final walk, just to say goodbye to the café and his life here on Mother Earth. It would have also been easier for him to catch a ride there, too, if he'd decided to go farther from Copper Canyon."

"Our dad walked off almost three years ago. The employees at that café aren't going to remember much now," Preston warned Rick.

"It's still worth a try," Rick said. "The fossil fuel industry in our state has grown these past few years, and a lot of oil and gas field workers take this highway to and from work. I've only passed the Totah a few times since returning, but there always seems to be several industry-associated vehicles parked there."

In a somber mood but with a solid plan now in mind, they set out to find answers.

Rick and Kim were the last to leave. Reaching the highway, he watched beyond the fences that paralleled the road. "There are a lot of sheep herders around here. Perhaps we can find some to talk to."

As the sun got higher in the sky, they saw an elderly Navajo woman sitting on a low hill, watching her goats and sheep.

"Let's go talk to her, if she's willing to speak with strangers. From the way she's dressed, and what she's doing, she's a Traditionalist. Do not mention skinwalkers," Rick warned.

"Got it."

They left the SUV parked on the side of the road and crossed the fence some distance from where the animals were grazing.

The woman turned to study them as they approached, her eyes narrowed, but seeing Rick, she relaxed.

"Do you know her?" Kim whispered.

"No, but she's probably heard of me," he answered. "If you hadn't noticed, there's a scar on my face."

He greeted the woman in the traditional way. "Aunt, do you have a moment?" Rick asked. "I'm the medicine man's foster son. His clan was the Salt People, and he was born for the Near the Water

People," Rick added, referring to his foster father's mother's clan, then his father's.

Normally he would have mentioned his own clan and that of his father's, but those were unknown to him. Considering no one had ever claimed him, he'd never been motivated enough to find out.

"I know who you are, nephew," she said with a nod. "It was a sad thing about the *hataalii*. His medicine was strong."

"Did you ever see him walking in this direction along the highway after leaving the canyon?"

"Many times. Then one day he stopped coming."

"Does anyone else pass by on a regular basis? Maybe another Navajo on his way to work or an oil worker?"

"Not that I've noticed," she said. "I visited with your father often because he was my friend. I also warned him not to accept rides with company men on their way to or from work. The days when we could trust people so easily were gone. He never worried, though."

They spoke for a little longer, but soon it became clear she had no more information to give him.

"Thank you, aunt," Rick said. As they headed back to the SUV, he added, "Let's go check out the Totah Café."

"What's 'Totah' mean?" she asked.

"Where three rivers meet. It's a place of rest."

They made their way back slowly, careful not to spook the sheep and goats.

With Rick leading the way, they went in and out a small arroyo recently formed by runoff. Rick stopped to pick something out of the small ditch. "What a rare find! I haven't seen one of these in years."

"What is it?"

"A flint arrowhead, probably made for hunting smaller animals, like rabbits." He showed it to her. It was small, gray, with one pointed end. "Flint is sacred to the Navajo. Our creation stories say it came from the hide of monsters that preyed on our land. It has power because of its hardness and its ability to reflect light."

He admired it for another minute, then handed it to her. "Carry it with you. Flint brings protection against evil."

She studied the arrowhead, noting two small notches toward the base, probably where leather sinew was wound, attaching it to the shaft of the arrow itself. The find had meant a great deal to him, yet he was giving it to her. "What a wonderful gift. Thank you."

"We'll get you a proper *jish* soon. That's a medicine pouch," he added.

They crossed the low wire fence, then were soon on their way to the café.

She thought of the qualities she'd always envisioned her ideal mate would have. She'd promised herself to find a romantic man who'd sweep her off her feet, one who'd bring her flowers for no reason at all…someone filled with surprises.

She looked over at Rick. This morning he'd surprised her by giving her something he valued, a gift far more precious than flowers he could have picked up anywhere. Today he'd given her a memory wrapped in flint.

THE CROWD INSIDE the Totah Café was sparse at the moment. Most of the customers were Navajo or Anglo oil workers who'd taken a coffee break between shifts. "Let's ask around quietly," Rick said. "I recognize the guy over there in the far booth, so we'll start with him."

As they moved across the room, Rick saw people glance at his face then quickly look away, as they often did.

From day one, Kim had been different. She'd never pitied him, nor made him feel different in any way. Kim saw him as a man—nothing more, nothing less.

"Donnie Atcitty," Rick said, looking at the man who was wearing a tan uniform, handgun and badge on his shirt that identified him as private security. "Haven't seen you since high school. Now you're carrying a weapon and working for Sunrise Energy."

"Yeah, I'm directing company security for over sixty company wells," Donnie replied, offering them a chair. After exchanging a few pleasantries, he focused on Rick. "I heard you were back and I've been meaning to pay you a visit. You back for good?"

"Yeah, that's the plan. For now, I'm staying at the ranch house with my brother and his wife."

"I was sorry to hear about your father, Rick. He was a good man."

Rick nodded. "We're still not sure what really happened to him, so now that I'm back, we're trying to piece things together. From what I've been told, he didn't appear to be sick."

"That's Anglo thinking," Donnie said, shaking his head. "Our people know when it's time to die, and they leave so that the house will be safe for the family. The *chindi* can make problems for the living, you know that."

"Are you a Traditionalist?" Kim asked him.

"Not me, but I'm married to a Traditionalist woman. The way I see it, it's about respecting old beliefs. You can accept the way things are here on the Rez, or not, but you can't change what is."

Kim nodded slowly.

"All true, but before I can let this go, I've got to make sure he walked off on his own free will, Donnie. You get me?"

"So that's what you're thinking," Donnie said in a quiet voice. "You may have a point. The old man made enemies, *hataaliis* often do, just like doctors or preachers."

Rick nodded. "I found out it was pretty cold the day he disappeared, so he may have hitched a ride. It's not unusual for an oil worker or truck driver to stop and lend a hand to someone on foot."

"I'll pass word among the crews and my staff via the radio net. But you're talking years ago, and we've got a lot of new people."

"I'd appreciate you giving it a try, Donnie. Here's my telephone number. You can reach me anytime. If you hear from anyone who remembers giving him a ride, give them my number. Hosteen Silver wasn't the kind anyone forgets. With that long silver hair of his, he was nothing if not memorable."

Donnie smiled. "No argument there." He stood. "Gotta go back to work. I hope you find the answers you need."

After a quick lunch, they climbed into the SUV and Rick dialed Kyle and Preston. Pressing the conference call button, he told them about his conversation with Atcitty.

"By the way," he said before ending the call, "do either of you know what happened to the rest of the books that were on the bookcase when I moved out?"

"You think the code's in one of those?" Preston asked almost immediately.

"It's a possibility. That's why I've got to track them down."

"Call Gene," Preston said. "He took quite a few of Hosteen Silver's books. He also made a list of the books we donated to the high school library."

"Okay, I'll talk to him."

Rick called Gene immediately.

"I did take them, and read quite a few, but I didn't keep them here. I stored them in a metal chest at the old cabin," Gene told him, referring to the place where he and Daniel had first lived when Hosteen Silver fostered them.

"I'll go up there and take a look. Spare key still under that flat rock?" he asked.

"Didn't think you still remembered after all these years," Gene answered.

"Hey, I love that place. I spent two weeks up there alone one winter break, remember?"

"I remember you burned up all the firewood," Gene recalled, chuckling.

After ending the call, Rick glanced at Kim. "I'd like to go right now. Any objections? The cabin's an hour west of here and north into the mountains. All in all, a very rough ride."

"Let's do it."

He started to switch directions when his phone rang.

"Mr. Cloud? My name's Larry Blake. I got your number from Donnie Atcitty. I'm calling about your father."

Chapter Fifteen

Rick arranged to meet Larry Blake and a friend of his, Victor Pete, who'd also seen Hosteen Silver that last day. The site of the meeting was to be the parking lot of a well-known trading post just off Highway 64, a few miles inside the Navajo Nation. Just to play it safe, Rick had asked Bidtah to run a background check on the men. Both had come up clean.

The drive took them about twenty minutes. As they pulled off the highway into the parking lot, they saw two men standing beside a pickup parked to one side of the lot. One man, an Anglo, was leaning against the truck bed, holding a can of soda in his gloved hand. The second man, a Navajo around five foot nine with a barrel chest, sat on the lowered tailgate, smoking a cigarette.

Rick pulled up and parked. "Stay alert," he told Kim.

"You're thinking it was too easy?"

"That, and I just don't like the looks of these guys."

"Oil and gas field workers are known for being tough. It comes with the job. I've met a few hard cases myself at the Brickhouse," Kim told him.

"All the more reason to be careful," Rick responded, stepping out of the SUV.

"Rick?" The Anglo came toward him and extended his hand. "Larry Blake. Victor and I gave your old man a ride that day. I remember because it was as cold as hell and he was just walking down the side of the road, real casual-like, his hair blowing in the wind."

A long silence stretched out, but Rick didn't interrupt. Anglos often felt uncomfortable during long pauses in the conversation and would begin talking just to fill the silence. He'd gotten his best leads that way over the years.

"From what I recall, he looked like he knew exactly what he was doing," Larry said. "When I asked him where he was headed on such a crappy day, he said he had some unfinished business. He asked us to take him as close to Big Gap as we could. That being several miles from the highway, in the middle of nowhere, I advised him to let us give him a ride home instead. It was getting stormy, and whatever business he had would wait until tomorrow, but he just shook his head."

"Where did you drop him off?"

"It was near one of the old oil wells about a mile from the highway in the Navajo Field."

"Show me."

"It's about forty-five minutes away, south of Shiprock, but Victor and I worked the graveyard shift, so we're done for the day."

"Good. I'll follow you," Rick said.

They rode east through the town of Shiprock, then south and west to an area filled with low hills and pines.

Rick followed Larry's pickup down a long, narrow, graveled road.

"What's bothering you?" Kim asked, no doubt picking up on his mood.

"I don't remember any oil wells this far off the highway. That's not to say there weren't any, because drilling has picked up in the past few years. Still, we should be watchful."

The road quickly deteriorated to nothing more than a few ruts across the desert. Ahead of them, the men in the pickup were bouncing around but refused to slow down. "It doesn't look like the oil companies ever did any drilling around here, or we would have seen some capped wells," Rick said. "I'm getting a bad feeling about this."

Just as he finished speaking, the truck ahead came to a stop. There was a wide arroyo ahead, blocking their way.

"Maybe they took a wrong turn," Kim suggested. "It's been a few years."

"Let's see what they have to say," Rick answered, climbing out of the SUV. Kim followed.

"Guys, sorry, I think I'm lost," Larry said, stepping out of the pickup. "This arroyo shouldn't be here."

"It happens," Rick said, shrugging. "Want to give it another try?"

Just then Victor came around the truck. He'd put on mirrored sunglasses and now had a pistol in his hand. "Bring out your weapon slowly, with your left hand, and drop it on the ground."

Rick, knowing he'd never be able to draw his pistol in time, did as he was asked. Silently, he noted that Larry didn't appear to have a handgun, though there was a long hunting knife in a sheath clipped on his belt.

"Now step back ten feet," Victor ordered, waving the barrel of his pistol back and forth.

Larry came forward, picked up Rick's weapon and stuck it into his waistband.

"Those sunglasses. *You* were the one who pushed the kitchen wall of the Brickhouse down on us," Kim said to Victor.

"Finally put that together, did you? You two are really hard to kill. I cut the gas line, blocked the exits, and you and the others still managed to get out without even a blister before the place went up in flames. Then I buried you under a ton of bricks and you tunneled your way out like prairie dogs," he said. "This is your third strike. Nothing personal, though. Larry and I are just the hired help. We never even met your old man."

"You plan on killing us, I get that. So why don't you tell us who's behind this?" Kim asked.

"Don't know, don't care," Victor answered. "Word got around at a cockfight up near Bloomfield that some local had enemies he wanted put down. I needed the money, so I stepped up and called the number. The voice was altered, but I said I'd do the job. An envelope was left for me at a drop site and inside was half the payment, photos and instructions. The party popper under the SUV was something special we added to the mix just to mess with you. Bet you jumped when it went off."

Rick ignored the comment. "So my foster father never came this way. It was all a con?" he asked, slowly moving away from Kim and edging closer to Victor. If he could take Victor's gun away from him, Kim could fend off Larry before he pulled his weapon. He'd seen her hand-to-hand skills.

"Once I heard the company security guy asking for help over the radio net, we made up stuff to draw you in."

"If anything happens to us, he'll know it was you," Kim pointed out.

Larry laughed. "Hey, all we have to say is you never showed up. And when nobody finds your bodies…"

Victor motioned with his pistol. "Enough talk. Walk over to the truck, slowly, hands away from your body. Don't try anything that'll get you killed before your time."

Larry reached the truck first and, bringing out two shovels from the bed, tossed them on the ground. "Pick them up and start digging." He pointed to the arroyo. "Find a soft spot if you want. The hole's got to be at least four feet deep and let's say six long."

"You want us to dig our own graves?" Kim demanded, sounding more outraged than scared. "Forget it! Dig them yourselves." She tossed the shovel down into the arroyo, then stepped back.

"Go get it—now!" Victor swung his handgun around, waving it at Kim.

Wielding the shovel like a bat, Rick connected with the pistol. Victor screamed in pain and the weapon went flying.

Larry looked down to grab Rick's pistol, which he'd tucked in his waistband, but Kim was already on the move. She dived at the man, who looked up in surprise, tried to dodge, then dropped the gun. Kim grabbed for it in midair, but missed and ended up knocking it into the arroyo.

Rick swung at Victor with the shovel again, but the guy blocked it with his arm, howling with pain. The handle broke and the shovel slipped from Rick's grip.

Victor reached down to his boot, no doubt for a backup pistol, but Rick, seeing the opening, attacked. With his left hand, Rick pinned Victor's neck, swinging him around toward Larry and using the man as a shield.

Rick reached down for Victor's small handgun, slipping off the safety with his thumb as he yanked it from the ankle holster and raised it toward the man.

Larry had managed to grab Kim, and now had the tip of his hunting knife next to her neck. "So what'll it be, Indian? Can you kill me before I cut her throat?" To make his point, he pressed the point of the blade into her neck until a drop of blood appeared.

Kim tried to lean away from the knife. "Take the shot!"

He should have done it. He was an excellent marksman. Yet the risk to Kim made it impossible for him to shoot. "I'm not letting your pal loose, or allowing you to walk away, either, Larry. Think hard, because you have one chance to live. If anything happens to her, you're next."

Kim suddenly went limp, collapsing out of Larry's grasp. As Larry tried to grab her, Rick squeezed the trigger. Larry fell to his knees, then onto his back, a bullet hole in the center of his forehead.

Victor elbowed Rick in the gut, twisting around

and reaching desperately for the pistol. As the weapon fell to the ground, Rick knocked Victor back with a stiff arm to the chest.

Rick turned for a brief second, trying to catch sight of the pistol, and then realized Victor had picked up Larry's knife.

This was one fight Rick had hoped to avoid. He wanted to take this guy in alive.

Victor slashed at him with the big blade, but Rick feinted left and dodged right, keeping his arms up to block any jab or sweeping motion.

Out of the corner of his eye, Rick saw Kim pick up the pistol. Before she could fire, Victor rushed Rick, jabbing the blade toward his gut.

Rick sidestepped, slipping outside the motion, and grabbed Victor's extended knife hand at the wrist and twisted. The man screamed in pain as bones cracked.

Rick kicked the man in the gut, then pushed him to the ground, overpowering him with a choke hold that quickly rendered Victor unconscious.

Rick rolled Victor so he was facedown and put his knee on the man's back. He looked over at Kim, who was now aiming the pistol at Victor.

"Find something to tie this guy up," he said, never easing his hold.

She looked into the back of the pickup and brought him a jumper cable. "No rope, but this should do."

After Victor was secured, Rick stood and quickly looked her over. "Are you okay?" Seeing the spot of blood on her neck, his gut tightened.

"I'm fine. It's just a scratch," she said, dabbing at the puncture wound with her hand. "It's already stopped bleeding."

Rick called Bidtah next and quickly filled him in, giving him directions and GPS coordinates. As soon as he ended the call, he looked back at her. "We're going to wait here for the tribal cops. Do you need to sit?"

She pulled down the pickup's tailgate and took a seat. "For a moment or two I thought that was it for both of us. Why didn't you take the shot?"

"I didn't have a clear line of fire," he said.

"Yet you were able to hit the exact spot you were aiming at while he was moving. When he had the knife at my throat, he was basically still, a much easier shot," she said.

"I couldn't risk hurting you," he said, grasping her shoulders and looking squarely at her. "Do you understand what I'm saying?"

She shook her head. "Talk to me. Help me understand you," she said, her voice unsteady for the first time.

"I care for you, Kim, more than I should. I'll do whatever I can to protect you, but you should run away from me. Go as far and as fast as you can. The man you see before you—that's only half the picture."

Before she could respond, they heard sirens coming up the road from the highway. He moved away from her. "That'll be Detective Bidtah and the Crime Scene Unit. They'll have a lot of questions, so get ready."

BIDTAH AND RICK stood aside, watching the Navajo M.E. and the other crime scene specialists work with the body.

"This is one of the cleanest shootings I've ever seen. One head shot, small caliber, instantly fatal. That's some marksmanship," Bidtah said.

"A necessary skill in my last occupation," Rick answered.

"We've got the deceased's address and we'll check out his place. I'll let you know what we find. We'll also be questioning Victor Pete at length. Preston will be present when we do," Bidtah added.

"Good."

Bidtah looked over at Kim, who joined them after having her small puncture wound photographed for the record. It had already stopped bleeding.

"If you're through with us here, I can take her to Copper Canyon and clean off her wound," Rick said.

"Go. I know where to find you," Bidtah answered.

As they walked back to the SUV, Rick caught a flicker of light coming from just beyond the highway. He hurried with her to the vehicle.

"What's going on?" she asked as they got under way.

"Someone's watching from that stand of cottonwoods we passed on the way in," Rick said. "It might just be a curious passerby who saw the tribal police and decided to take photos to post on the internet."

"Or not. You going to tell Bidtah?"

"Yeah, but I also intend to check things out for myself." He slowed, brought out his cell phone and called Bidtah.

Several seconds later Rick ended the call and looked over at Kim. "He's sending one of his officers." He brought out his pistol and placed it on the seat between them. "You up to this again, so soon?"

"You bet. Let's go."

He smiled. He loved her spirit.

Chapter Sixteen

They drove past the grove of trees and parked out of sight around a curve in the road. On foot, they advanced quietly, circling around from the opposite side of the stand of cottonwoods. Rick finally stopped about fifty yards from where he'd seen the flicker of light. Using the binoculars he'd pulled from the glove compartment, he searched the low, marshy area carefully. "No one's there now, but I'd like to take a look around anyway."

They walked up a small wash that drained the marshy spot—Rick was alert every step of the way—but there was very little ground cover. Soon he caught a flicker of motion to his left.

"Officer Sells," the man said, immediately identifying himself and stepping out from where he'd been crouching beside a juniper. "I swept the area coming in from the west at the other end of this wash. Subject's gone. Wanna take a look?"

Rick followed Sells to the location and saw a small medicine bag lying on the ground. It was made of the skins of horned toads. "That's a witch bag," he explained to Kim. "It's the opposite of a medicine bag." He paused, gathering his thoughts. "The flicker of light, whether it came from a mirror, rifle scope or binoculars, was no accident. Someone wanted us to find this. It's a way of saying they're not through yet."

Officer Sells radioed Bidtah, explaining that they'd found no shoe or boot prints, just faint moccasin impressions.

"Someone sure hates you," Sells told Rick after ending the transmission.

"Yeah, but they don't know me very well. If anything, this just makes me more determined to find them."

Sells nodded, then began the walk back to the crime scene.

Once inside the SUV, Rick gazed at her for a long moment. "If you're in this for the duration, so be it, Kim, but you'll need to carry the right weapons."

"I qualified with several infantry weapons in the army, including handguns," she said.

"Not those kinds of weapons."

"You're referring to traditional Navajo protection, like fetishes and medicine bags, aren't you?" she asked.

"Yes. It'll show respect for our culture and traditions, which means people on the Rez will be more likely to trust you. It'll be late by the time we get there, but Pablo Ortiz lives at the rear of his store. He'll welcome us even if it's after hours for him."

"Mr. Ortiz of Southwest Treasures?"

He smiled as they drove east toward Hartley. "You know him?"

"Only by name."

They pulled into the rear parking lot of Southwest Treasures instead of parking at the curb.

As Rick got down from the SUV, Pablo Ortiz, a short, rotund Zuni tribesman with gray hair and a wide smile, came out to greet them.

"Welcome, Rick! You picked a great time to visit. After hours is always best. No interruptions."

After Rick introduced Kim to Pablo, they went inside and Pablo led them up the stairs into a tiny kitchen.

"My friend needs a *jish* and a special fetish. She's helping me on a case," Rick said.

"Then come with me into my work area." He took them into the small living room. At the center of the room beneath a bright overhead light was a sofa, a leather recliner and a metal tray with various grinding and polishing tools.

Following her line of sight, Ortiz smiled. "My special pieces are finished there, but the initial work requires a more secure surface." He pointed to a bigger wood table on the north side of the room.

Above it was a shelf containing handsaws, mallets, chisels and stone rasps and files of all sizes.

"I have three finished fetishes. I don't know who they'll go to yet, but the spirit inside the stone will know its owner."

Kim walked over to the larger table. "Is it okay for me to take a closer look?"

"Go ahead," Ortiz said.

"We were looking for a—" Rick started but grew silent when Ortiz held up his hand.

The first fetish was a small bear made of jet. The second was a beautiful blue-turquoise lizard. The third was a horse made of alabaster, with a turquoise heart line etched from its mouth to its heart. Feathers adored its back.

"This one is gorgeous," she said.

Ortiz smiled at Rick, then glanced back at her. "Horse chooses you, as you've chosen it," he said.

"What do the feathers stand for?" she asked.

"They are an offering to the spirit of the fetish and increase its power. Feathers, blue ones in particular, are powerful medicine."

Ortiz looked at her for a moment. "What led you to choose Horse?"

She told him about Hosteen Silver's note, adding, "This one reminded me of fearlessness and freedom." She looked at the small figure in her palm.

Ortiz smiled. "Good. The match is complete."

"Thank you, uncle," Rick said. "We'll also need a *jish,* one with protective qualities."

His uncle walked across the room and picked up a small leather bag from a collection of five. "This has pollen, a crystal and a sprig from a powerful good luck plant. It's perfect for Horse and you," he said, handing it to Kim.

She carefully placed the small fetish in her pouch and, following Ortiz's directions, sprinkled it with pollen. Then after asking permission, she added the flint arrowhead to its contents.

Rick paid the customary amount and Pablo Ortiz thanked him. "Be careful, both of you. Something tells me you've yet to face your worst enemy."

"Thank you for the warning, uncle. We'll remember," he said.

As they left, heading back to the Rez, Kim felt different somehow. "Thank you for this," she said, her hand on the small pouch now attached to her belt. "It was pretty amazing how your foster father mentioned Horse, and the right one was here waiting for me."

"Pablo's got an instinct for things of this nature. I was the hardest to read of all my brothers. Even Hosteen Silver was unsure which fetish would be right for me, so he brought me here. We stayed for several hours, shared a meal and just talked. Pablo wanted to know what my plans for the future were."

"How old were you?"

"Sixteen, but even back then I knew what I wanted. I told him I needed to lead a life with a clear purpose. One where I'd be challenged and each day was different from the last. My goal, even back then, was to join a federal agency and do undercover work."

"So you became someone else for a while and brought some bad people to justice. Yet the act of surviving isn't the same as living life, either."

He looked at her for a moment and then focused his eyes on the highway. The SUV's headlight beams were quickly swallowed up by the yawning black void ahead. The only other lights were stars in the dry desert sky.

"Rick, no warrior wears his armament all the time."

She wanted to reach him, to connect. She understood why he'd closed himself off, yet she knew he'd never find happiness until he learned how to lower his guard and let people in.

Silence ensued but she didn't press him. Looking around into the darkness surrounding the SUV made her feel claustrophobic. "I've lost track of where we are and where we're going," she said at last.

"My foster father's old cabin. I have a feeling that the code I need is inside one of the books Gene is storing up there."

"Tell me more about the cabin," she said. "What can I expect?"

"Daniel and Gene lived there with Hosteen Silver the first year they came to stay with him. It's small, just two rooms, and when they arrived there was no running water. They had to carry containers uphill from a well that was near a spring on the property."

"Even a few gallons of water are heavy. That would have been a tough workout."

"Yeah it was, but Hosteen Silver saw it as a way of making the guys too tired to stir up trouble. They were both pretty wild back then, so he'd decided to challenge them and teach them to work together."

"Did you have heat?" she asked. "A woodstove or anything?"

"There's a woodstove for cooking and a well-designed fireplace. The temperature tonight will go down into the low forties, so I'll make a fire as soon as we get there and warm us up. Since Daniel uses the cabin when he goes hunting, we've added a generator and electricity."

"And running water?"

"Just cold, and trust me when I say *cold*."

She smiled. "We can heat some up on the stove if necessary."

Almost two hours later, Rick pulled up to a

wood cabin in the middle of a small clearing a few miles inside the pine forest.

It took a few minutes to find the key, but they were soon inside the solid-looking log structure with its corrugated metal roof.

Kim looked around. It was small, yet despite the frigid temperature in the room, had the comfy feel of an oasis, a touch of civilization in the middle of the wilderness. It was furnished simply, just a couch and one easy chair, but the beautiful, cream-colored sheepskin rug by the fire caught her eye. It looked incredibly soft and fit the cabin's rustic atmosphere.

"I'm going to build a fire," Rick announced. "My brother stacks the wood next to the generator shed, so I'll turn the electricity on while I'm out there."

As he left, she kept her gloves and coat on to ward off the chill, and looked around. There were no photos on the walls, but on the desk near the corner there was a framed photo of Holly, Daniel's wife, holding a baby.

After Rick came back in, she watched him start the fire, using wadded-up newspapers to get the kindling lit in a hurry. Rick moved with purpose and confidence, the quintessential man.

Once the fire was going, he glanced up at her. "You're freezing, aren't you?" he asked, standing to full height again.

She'd wrapped her arms around herself tightly; her gloves were still on. "Guilty," she said with a tiny smile. "My heavy coat is still at my apartment."

He came over and, opening his own jacket, pulled her against him.

The gesture had been completely unexpected and took her by surprise. Nestled against him and his warmth, she felt protected, secure. She loved feeling his heartbeat against her. He was strong and steadfast, and she melted against his rock-solid chest.

He tilted her chin up and kissed her tenderly. "You're safe with me—always."

His heat was intoxicating. "I just wish…"

"What? You can tell me anything, you know that, don't you?

"You've told me before that I don't see the real you, Rick, but how can I, when you won't let me in? You want me to trust you, to lose myself in your arms. I want that, too, but you've put up a wall between us," she whispered. "Let go. Trust me, just as I trust you."

He didn't ease his hold. He kept her pressed against him. "I learned to protect myself by keeping everyone at bay. It was the only way I knew to keep life from kicking me in the gut. As time went by I guess those instincts became part of who I am."

"It's a good enough way to live if you plan on spending your life alone, but most of us want more than that."

"I wanted no part of love. At best it's an illusion, a fantasy that quickly fades. At its worst, it's a tool used to manipulate people you care about."

"But you're close to your brothers. You love them."

"What binds us are loyalty, integrity and honor. Those attitudes—commitments—are more reliable than romantic love."

"For those to remain strong, they have to be rooted in love," she murmured, her face nestled against his neck.

"I have feelings for you, Kim, the kind you can always count on. I'll be there for you no matter what," he said, easing his hold and brushing his palm against the side of her face.

"But you're still fighting this. Why?"

"Because of what I see in your eyes when you look at me."

"I don't understand."

"You see who you want me to be, not who I really am."

"What I see is the man who protected me, who shielded me with his own body. You saved my life."

"And took others," he said. "I'm not a choir boy."

"What you are is a man who'll risk everything to

do what's right, one who isn't afraid of anything—except letting people get close," she said. "But for us to have more than just a snapshot in time, you have to open your heart."

He released her and stepped back. "Kim, there are things about me you don't want to hear. Once they're said, we'll never be able to go back to the way things are now."

"You care for me, but you'll never trust my feelings for you until you stop keeping me at arm's length."

Rick nodded slowly. "All right." He brushed a kiss on her forehead and moved farther away. Restless, he began to pace, his hands jammed deep into the pockets of his leather jacket. "I thought I was perfect for undercover work—cold, focused and able to think on the fly, but there was more to the job. White hats versus black hats are a myth. There are many shades of gray. The longer you're in, the more you understand bad guys are seldom totally evil."

He ran a hand through his close-cropped hair, struggling to find the right words. "When you begin to see parts of yourself in the people you're there to bring down, you start to question what you're doing. That's when things begin to unravel."

"So why didn't you ask to be pulled out?"

"It had taken me more than a year to infiltrate that human trafficking cartel, and my work was finally providing valuable intel—names, places and events. I was real close to shutting down the entire operation," he said, staring into the fire.

Minutes passed, but she didn't interrupt. Some things couldn't be forced.

"Then the head of the cartel ordered me to kill a man—his competitor, another trafficker. I would have been doing the world a favor, but I wasn't there to do the cartel's dirty work."

He shook his head and rubbed the back of his neck. "I made the decision to let fate handle the outcome. I arranged a meet, knowing he'd try to kill me and that only one of us would walk away. Self-defense was something I could live with."

Another silence ensued before he continued. "We met in a church parking lot, which turned out to be an ambush. I was set up. A wedding was going on inside, so he'd planned to use a knife instead of a gun. It was a brutal fight. The man was strong and fast—a former soldier. My training was better, though. Soon I had him pinned against the side of a car. I was about to finish him off when he looked directly at me—helpless."

Rick turned away from her to lean against the brick fireplace and stare out the window.

She came over to him and placed her arm around his waist.

He turned and held on to her. "It wasn't until I

saw myself reflected in that man's eyes that I realized what I'd become. I'd wanted to kill him and had been looking for justification. I pulled back, intending to let him go, but he grabbed his fallen knife and took the swipe that gave me this scar. Then he moved in for the kill. In the end, I survived, he didn't."

"You did what you had to do," she said. "You gave him a chance. Your humanity came through."

"And it nearly cost me my life. As I walked to my car, half-blinded by the blood, his bodyguard stepped out of hiding and shot me three times. A few seconds later, a local cop took him down.

"Later, in the hospital between surgeries, I had plenty of time to think about what I wanted to do next. I decided to come home and reconnect with myself. Figuring once I was back on my turf, I'd be able to find a new purpose for myself, a reason to get up in the morning."

"And the mystery behind your father's disappearance has given you that?"

"No, *you* did," he said. Tilting her chin up, he kissed her slowly and tenderly.

When Rick released her, a small tremor ran up her spine. "You've gone through hell, Rick, but you're a man of honor and compassion. You're everything I thought you were—and more."

He kissed her hard then, forcing her lips to part for him as he drank her in.

FIRE COURSED THROUGH HER. She'd met men over the years who'd attracted her, but she'd never felt this overwhelming need to give her love without demands or conditions. Maybe real love didn't need a reason, just the freedom to exist.

Though Rick hadn't said he loved her, it didn't seem to matter now. She pushed his jacket back and opened his shirt, wanting to feel his muscled chest. As she looked up at him, she saw the dark fire in his eyes. He was holding back, keeping a tight rein on himself. His jaw was clenched, and as she left a moist trail down his chest, he sucked in his breath.

There were two scars on his chest, both up high, by his collarbone. Below, over his heart, was a Navajo word: *Chaha'oh*. She ran her fingertips over it. "What's it mean?"

"Shadow. That's what many claimed I was like when I hunted man or beast."

She kissed his scars one by one and felt him shudder. When she moved to unbuckle his belt, he placed his hand over hers. "It's not too late to change your mind, but it will be in another second or two."

"Rick, I'm not afraid of you. Open your heart to me. Let me show you that love doesn't have to hurt."

She undid his belt and caressed him.

"Slow down," he whispered, pulling her hands

up and placing them on his chest. He slipped off her jacket, then tugged at her sweater and pants until she stood naked by the fire. Lifting her into his arms, he lowered her onto the sheepskin rug.

In the flickering firelight, a world of light and shadows, they came together. Heat became a living force. The roughness of his touch drove her wild. This was love—and their destiny.

She knew Rick struggled to maintain control for as long as he could. Yet the fire coursing through him seemed to increase with each second. With a groan, he surrendered and completed what was meant to be.

Even after their breathing evened, Kim held on to him, refusing to let him move away. "For now, you're mine and I'm yours. Don't go."

"I'm here."

Chapter Seventeen

Time passed and the air in the room began to grow cold.

"The fire's almost out," Rick said, moving away from Kim's arms and getting dressed. "Too bad it's not summer. I would have loved seeing you walk around naked."

"You're not so bad yourself," she said, her gaze taking him in slowly.

He laughed. "Scarred and worn, but not too bad?"

"I've got no complaints," she said, reaching for her clothes.

He gave her a hand up. "We'll warm up sooner if we get to work. Let's find the books and take them out to the SUV. I'm not leaving them here. This place doesn't have the electronic protection the ranch does," he said. "More importantly, we don't know who else knows of this place besides family."

"Did your brother tell you where he put the books?"

"No, just that they're in a metal trunk. I don't see

them here, and they weren't in with the generator, so I'm sure they're in the bedroom," he said, gesturing with his head toward the door.

"I can't remember ever being this cold," she said, wrapping the sides of her jacket tightly around herself.

"I do, but it was a long time ago," he admitted. "Once I get the fire going again, it'll heat up fast. Don't worry, I can build a fire in the stove, as well. Daniel's a wuss about cold, so he sold the old potbellied stove and added this beauty." He pointed toward the steel stove with its two big doors, the right one with a glass window. "No gas, no electricity, just firewood in the left side."

"Daniel doesn't seem like a wuss to me," she said, laughing.

"Well, he is. Just don't tell him I said so. He's the one who paid for the upgrades."

A short while later they'd pulled two large boxes from a big trunk in the bedroom. They were clearly labeled Books and marked with the date they'd been packed. "That's Gene. He's organized about everything," Rick said.

They carried the boxes into the main room and placed them on the heavy pine table. "I want to sort through these before we load them into the SUV. I'm not taking back any passengers, like mice, to my brother's house."

"Yeah, I saw the chewed corner," Kim said.

"He must have kept the boxes outside the trunk at one time."

Rick opened the flaps of the first box and reached for a fat, clearly water-damaged paperback that had long lost its cover. "I remember this one. It's signed by one of the Navajo Code Talkers, a man Hosteen Silver greatly admired. Kyle was reading it one summer and accidentally dropped it into the horse tank. I helped Hosteen Silver dry it out, but it looked ruined to me. Since he'd read it a million times, I assumed he'd chucked it," he said, leafing through the loose, brittle pages until he found something of interest. "There's a torn page from another book stuck in here at the halfway point. It's from a book about Richard Sorge, from what I can tell."

"Who's Richard Sorge?" Kim said.

"Don't know. Once we have internet access, we can do a search. If the code I found in the notebook is based on a book about, or by, Sorge, maybe we're on to something."

She helped him return the books to the box before they opened the other one. "You want to go directly to Daniel's place instead of to the ranch house? Paul and Daniel seem to know more about codes than Kyle."

"Yeah, let's go to Daniel's. I have a feeling we're close to answering some important questions."

He doused the fire and they locked up the cabin, loading the boxes into the SUV.

Rick took it slow as they went down the narrow road, which was basically a bumpy trail cut into the hillside by vehicle use, not road equipment. After a quarter of a mile, needing to slow before crossing a dip in the road, he touched the brake.

"The brakes feel spongy," he said in a taut voice, his hands clenching the wheel. "Not good."

The SUV bounced hard as they crossed the shallow trench. Kim grabbed the armrest and adjusted her seat belt.

"We've lost our brakes," Rick said. He pulled the handbrake and it grabbed, slowing them a little. "Hold on," he said, turning the wheel slightly to the right and trying to skid to a stop as he reapplied the handbrake.

The SUV rocked to the left and the right rear tire rose off the ground. When he swerved left, the wheel touched down again. Even though they bounced heavily, the road was steep and they picked up speed once more.

He glanced over at her. Kim had pressed her back against the seat, her eyes wide with fear as she hung on to the armrest.

Ahead was the steepest part of the trail, a sharp curve and a fifty foot drop to the left. At the speed they were going, Rick knew he wouldn't be able to hold the turn. They'd fly right over the edge.

For a second he thought a forced roll would be safer—they were buckled in and the air bags would help. Then he remembered the brush ahead. There was still a chance...

"Hang on, this is going to get rough," he yelled, veering off the road to the right and ramming into a scrub oak thicket about three feet high. The soft impact knocked him into the steering wheel, enough to cost him a breath, but not enough to trigger the air bag.

Rick hung on to the wheel, whipping it back and forth, fishtailing as they rammed their way through the thicket, racing up slope. There was a loud, jarring thump somewhere underneath them and Kim bounced into the air, bumping her head on the roof.

Their speed dropped and the rear wheels grabbed on to something. As the SUV slid to a stop, dust enveloped them in a cloud.

Rick reached down and turned off the ignition. The engine rattled for a few seconds. The front end vibrated. Then suddenly it was dead quiet.

After a second Rick's ears stopped ringing and he looked over at Kim.

She smiled weakly. "Are we there yet?"

"Take it as a win. This may be as far as we can go, but at least we're in one piece." He looked around carefully before glancing back at her. "Stay in the vehicle for now. I'm going to take a look underneath to see if I can figure out what happened."

"No, I'm going with you. I can hold the flashlight while you check the brakes. I can also keep an eye out for anyone who might be lurking about. This may not have been an accident," she said, climbing out her side.

Rick crawled beneath the SUV and studied the damage. "From the smell of brake fluid and the crimp in the line, which is now dangling loose, you're right. This was done on purpose." When he came back out and stood, his jaw was set. "I let my guard down, Kim, and brought this on. I'm sorry."

"I don't understand. How is this—" She stopped abruptly. "You mean because we made love?"

"I was on the job. I should know better than to get so distracted."

"First, you don't know exactly when the person sabotaged that brake line except that it was after we arrived. We may have been searching for the books at the time, or maybe it was done right after we arrived and you were busy building a fire," she protested.

"More importantly," she added softly, "I wouldn't trade a second of what happened between us." She held his gaze. "It drew us closer, and if you allow it, it'll make us even stronger."

He smiled. "You look like an angel, but you've got a core of steel, Kim."

"Most women do," she answered.

He studied the area around him, taking everything in slowly and thoroughly. "Escape and evasion. I'm trained for this. Let's get moving, in case whoever did this stuck around to watch. There's a tool bag in the back. Let's empty it out and put the books inside. I'll carry it while you take the binoculars in the glove compartment. They're infrared."

"Okay."

"It's a half-hour hike to the main road. Once we're there I'll be able to get a cell phone signal. I'll call Daniel and let my brothers know what happened. Preston will be able to get the tribal police moving on this. There's no second set of tracks on the road, so the guy must have approached on foot. His vehicle is probably parked in the vicinity."

Rather than stick to the trail, they moved directly downhill, sticking to cover whenever possible to avoid being spotted. Rick scarcely made a sound even through the rough terrain, but Kim knew she was probably alerting wild animals for miles.

"Do you think the person's still out there? They haven't done anything directly, like shoot at us," she noted. "Not yet anyway," she added, looking over her shoulder.

"My gut tells me our enemy is around here somewhere. There's no way for him to have predicted how effective tampering with the brakes would be. Once he sees we've walked away unhurt, he'll probably try something else."

DANIEL PICKED THEM up at the highway and before long they were inside Daniel's office in the computer room, all holding freshly brewed hot coffee. Preston had just arrived and Paul was already behind the computer.

"Let me look up Richard Sorge for you. Then we can go from there," Paul said, typing in the name.

He then looked up at them. "He ran a Soviet spy ring in Japan before and during World War II. They used OTPs—one time pads—that required both sender and recipient to have the identical page to decipher the message. Although it was more secure than what the code talkers used, it was also a lot more time-consuming to decode," he said. "Do you still have the photos of the code you found in the notebook Hosteen Silver left for you?"

"Yes, I do." Rick handed Paul his cell phone and Paul transferred the images to the central screen.

"They're sequences of numbers separated by commas," Daniel said. "But it isn't a simple grade-school code, where the number one equals *a,* two equals *b* and so forth. We've already checked some of those patterns."

"A common substitute for those OTPs is one that requires both sender and receiver to have identical editions of the same book—a popular novel, reference book, even a dictionary. If we can find the book our father used to create the code, we can figure out the message," Paul concluded.

Rick studied the well-worn paperback in his hands. Although they'd looked for a book about Sorge, it hadn't been in either box. "I think he mentioned Sorge to tell us he was using a variation of the old-style OTP code," Rick said. "Let's check the books, starting with his favorite, and see what we get."

"Go from the premise that the first number corresponds to the page, the second is the line number, the third is the word and the fourth is the letter in the word," Paul said.

Rick checked the old paperback and followed the sequence. "First letter is an *s*." A few minutes later Rick looked up and smiled. "First word is *she*. Second is *fed*. Third word is *it*."

"That can't be a coincidence," Kim said, looking from brother to brother. "*She fed it* is not random. And the only woman who's a suspect in all this is Angelina Curley."

Rick nodded and continued matching numbers with letters, writing them down. "The next word is *to*. Last word…" He paused. "There's water damage on this page, but I think the last word is *me*."

"*She fed it to me.*" Kim looked around the room. "What did Angelina feed your father?"

"This was in a notebook with information about

the Plant People, so I think Hosteen Silver was trying to tell us he was poisoned," Rick said.

"He hid that notebook in a place only you would find," Kim said. "I think it's safe to assume he was concerned his enemy, probably Angelina, would sweep the ranch house to make sure no evidence of what she'd done was left behind."

"What I don't get is why he didn't call you, Preston, or the tribal police, and identify Angelina," Daniel interjected. "Or just name his killer outright."

"Maybe he wasn't one hundred percent sure, and didn't want to make what was essentially a death-bed statement, naming the wrong killer," Kim suggested.

"He may also have known help wouldn't arrive in time, or that nothing could be done, so he used his remaining energy to do what he felt was honorable—die as far away from his home as possible," Paul said.

"Or maybe he thought he might be able to reach Angelina in time and she'd have the plants necessary for an antidote," Daniel said. "But, as Kim suggested, that doesn't necessarily make her guilty. She might have simply shared his love for the Plant People."

"But Angelina doesn't live anywhere near Copper Canyon," Kim pointed out.

"This all happened before she married," Paul

responded. "Let's see where she lived before then. Hang on." Paul typed something into his computer and a minute later looked up. "According to MVD records, Angelina lived just three miles from Copper Canyon. It's possible that since his truck wouldn't start, our foster father set out on foot to her house but never made it."

"Great theory, but without a body, we still have zero," Preston conceded. "We can't prove how he died or even that he *is* dead."

"There's something that still doesn't make sense to me," Kim said. "Why would Angelina try to kill Rick after all this time? Even if she did kill Hosteen Silver, she'd already gotten away with murder. No body, no witnesses, no real evidence except the coded message—and that doesn't identify her, not really."

There was a long silence as everyone considered the possibilities.

"She may have been afraid that once Rick was back, he'd somehow be able to tie the poisoning to her," Preston said. "Rick was the only one of us who could think like Hosteen Silver. That's scarcely a secret."

"Makes sense, but finding the body is totally up to us now," Daniel said. "We need to hike away from the ranch house to the location of Angelina's former home. We should take the most likely direct routes, and search along those trails. If he didn't make it to her place, his body has to be around there somewhere."

Paul used his computer to locate an aerial view of the area, and showed the others what was on the monitor.

"The shortest route passes through a section with no homes or signs of habitation. Just nature and wild animals," Preston observed, not needing to explain the gruesome possibilities. "His body may be long gone by now."

"We still have to do this, and we can't depend on help from anyone else," Paul said. "No Navajo would go searching for a body under these circumstances, at least no Traditionalist."

"Let's get a few hours of sleep, then start first thing in the morning," Rick said, stifling a yawn. "Kim, we'd all understand if you want to sit this one out."

"Give me a good strong cup of coffee and I'll be ready when you guys are," she answered.

Rick's phone rang. "It's two in the morning. This can't be good."

Chapter Eighteen

Rick identified himself to the caller and immediately recognized the rough voice at the other end.

"It's Ray," he said, no longer using "Mike," the name Kim had given him. "Detective Bowman let word out that he was looking for Nestor Sandoval and I've found him. He's in Hartley, lying low, but I know where he is."

"Give me the address," Rick said quickly.

"The numbers aren't there anymore, but it's the abandoned building behind the gas station on Pine. The station is closed for the night but there's a light in the alley. I saw Sandoval go in through the back. He hasn't left, so he must still be inside. He's also alone, from what I can tell."

"How do you know Sandoval?" Rick asked.

"He's the guy I bought a combat knife from—a KA-BAR. I needed a weapon to defend myself if it came to that," Ray answered.

"Can you keep an eye on the place until we get there?" Rick asked.

"I'll stay here by the pay phone and follow him if he leaves."

"Observe, but don't engage. Is that clear?" Rick said crisply.

"Copy," Ray answered, all business now, as if the soldier in him had awoken. "Avoid approaching using the street north of the station. He's placed boards with nails and broken glass all over the ground to discourage visitors."

"You know a better way in?"

"Affirmative," Ray replied. "Approach from the east and circle south around the gas station. That'll screen your approach and place you on the east side of the house. There's a vacant lot full of weeds there, and no road access, so he won't expect anyone to come from that direction. You'll have darkness on your side, as well."

"Good job, soldier," Rick said, then ending the call, filled everyone in.

"I can call for police backup," Preston said, "but going through channels will come at a cost. You all know I prefer to go by the book, but this may be our last chance to get Sandoval. I don't think we can afford to wait for SWAT and risk losing the element of surprise."

"Then let's move," Rick said.

"He won't come easily," Daniel said. "He's facing three strikes now."

"At least there's less risk to the public. That area

is commercial and industrial and at this hour nobody should be around. We'll do what we have to," Preston said.

"I've seen combat, I can help," Kim said.

"No. This is an entirely different situation, and there are different rules to follow," Preston said.

"Why don't you come and watch our backs in case someone tries to sneak up behind us?" Rick asked.

"Consider it done," she answered.

PAUL WAS ASSIGNED to cover the northern approach, a likely escape route for Sandoval considering he knew where he'd placed the obstructions. Rick and Preston would approach from the east, as advised, while Daniel moved in from the southwest corner to prevent any exit south. There were no west-facing windows or doors.

They all carried radios with earplugs, remaining in constant contact as they advanced. There was a full moon, so they wouldn't be groping around in the dark, at least.

Rick reached the east wall of the single-story building first, staying low to avoid being seen from any of the building's windows. Preston was to his right, farther north along the same wall. Each was approaching a window. The plan was for one of them to enter through whichever opening offered the easiest access, while the other provided cover.

Rick noticed a heating unit on the ground close to the southernmost window and silently pointed it out to Preston. He then contacted Kim, who was back at the corner of the garage, watching both north and south with infrared binoculars provided by Daniel.

"You're all still clear," she said.

"I'm going in," he whispered into the radio before climbing onto the unit and through the window.

A minute later he was crouched low beside the open doorway of the room he'd entered, listening and watching the hall as Preston climbed in. The room was unlit, but the moon was bright, the windows large and the walls light-colored. There was no way he'd miss seeing a man-size figure. As his brother lowered himself onto the floor, his shoe landed on a chunk of glass, making it crunch loudly.

Rick turned and waved him toward the corner just as footsteps raced down the hall. Aiming a pistol into the room from out in the hall, Sandoval fired blindly, not presenting a target. Two bullets hit the wall beside the window.

Rick shifted his aim, but the shooter's pistol, which had been barely three feet from him, disappeared before he could acquire a target.

"Go," Preston ordered over the radio, signaling for Paul and Daniel to close in. There was the sound of footsteps as Sandoval ran down the hall.

"Police! Put down your weapon and give up before you get hurt!" Preston called out. "The building's surrounded."

"I'm not going back to prison," Sandoval yelled from somewhere inside.

Rick took a quick look out to his left, seeing only a blind corner, and stepped into the hall, hugging the far wall. Weapon aimed, he looked over at Preston.

"Got your back," Preston whispered.

Rick inched down the wall to the corner, ducked low and took a quick look. Sandoval was crouched behind a stack of wood pallets, his pistol aimed right at him. Rick ducked back just in time. Two bullets came his way, one taking a chunk out of the corner.

Rick leaped across the hall and through an open doorway, firing toward the pallets as he moved. Once inside the room, he glanced around. It was empty and smelled of mold and damp wood, probably the results of a leaky roof.

From his position near the door, Rick looked back at Preston and nodded, ready to provide cover.

Preston crept to the corner where Rick had been just seconds earlier and looked up at the shot-out chunk of masonry.

"Move in carefully, guys. I'm going to draw his fire," Preston whispered over the radio. "I got a look at his weapon. It's a revolver. Two more rounds and he has to reload."

Preston stuck out his pistol and then pulled it back.

Sandoval fired once, hitting the wall.

Rick put his pistol back in its holster and looked across the way at Sandoval. He'd turned to look out a north window just as Preston fired two more shots, striking one of the pallets.

Sandoval fired back, then Rick heard a click. Sandoval was out of ammo.

Rick rushed into the room, leaped across the pallets and tackled Sandoval.

Sandoval went down, Rick on top. In a matter of seconds Preston was there, along with Daniel and Paul, both carrying bright flashlights to illuminate the scene. By then Sandoval was on his back and Rick had pinned him to the floor.

Preston cuffed him and read him his rights. "Come on. I'm taking you in."

"You know who we are?" Daniel asked Sandoval.

"Yeah, and you think I had something to do with the explosion at the restaurant," he said, looking at Rick.

"Let me guess. You're completely innocent," Rick said.

Sandoval stood as Preston held on to his arm. "No one over the age of five is completely innocent."

"Did you know what was going down or not?" Rick prompted.

"Hell, no. I had nothing to do with your old man's disappearance. I do have information to trade, if you're willing to cut me a deal."

"Let's go to the station," Preston snapped, leading him out the north side toward Main Street. "We'll talk there."

RICK WATCHED PRESTON get into his cruiser, parked at the curb one block down from the gas station, and drive off. Paul and Daniel left next.

Rick met Kim at the SUV, which had been next to Paul and Daniel's vehicle. "Have you seen Ray?" he asked.

"Not since we arrived."

"I'd like to try to find him."

"He probably didn't go far. We'll have better luck on foot," she said.

They set out together, walking down the alley on the north side of Main Street. They'd gone halfway down the block when Ray stepped out of the shadows. "Looking for me?"

The change in him was subtle, but nonetheless there. He stood straight, his gaze steady.

"Sure am, Ray. We wanted to tell you personally how much we appreciate your help tonight."

"No prob, and thanks to you guys, too. You reminded me what it was like to have something important to do again," he said. "I got in touch with an organization that helps local vets. Now I have a place to sleep and a job. As it turned out, one of the volunteers over at Warriors in Transition is an old friend. He runs a dog-training operation at the edge of town. He and I were both handlers and loved working with the dogs," Ray said. "He's invited me to teach basic obedience classes for problem dogs."

"Congratulations," Rick said, shaking his hand.

"Me, too, Ray," Kim said softly.

As Ray walked off, Rick smiled. "The man's taking control of his life again. He'll be okay now."

"I think so, too," she said. "You made a real difference when you treated him like an equal and asked for his help."

"Everyone needs a hand at one point or another. I'm glad I was there. The road back is tough, but the first step is the hardest."

Rick walked with her to the SUV. "Let's go find out what Sandoval's holding back."

"Do you think Preston's going to offer him a deal?"

"Eventually, but first he'll want to make sure the information is worth it."

KIM WAS LOOKING through the two-way glass, listening to what was going on in the interrogation room. Preston and Rick had gone inside and Daniel had gone home, but Paul was keeping her company.

"My brother has strong feelings for you, Kim," he said. "I've never seen him relax around anyone except us—until now. He needs you."

"I need him, too," she said quietly. "If you're worried I'll hurt him, please don't be. What we have isn't exactly Romeo and Juliet, but it is right for us."

He nodded. "Good to hear."

Looking at Sandoval, who was handcuffed to a table, they focused on what was being said inside.

"I want full immunity," Sandoval said. "Give me that and I'll steer you in the right direction."

"Do you know who cut the gas line at the Brickhouse?" Preston demanded.

Kim looked over at Paul. They already knew that answer.

"Patience," Paul whispered. "Preston is good at this."

"No, but I've got a pretty good idea who was behind it and why," Sandoval responded.

"Keep talking. We need to know that what you have is worth something," Preston said.

He shook his head. "No way. You first."

"Okay, I'll drop the charges for attempted assault on a police officer," Preston said. "Your turn."

"No weapons charge, either," Sandoval said.

Preston shrugged. "*If* what you've got leads to a conviction on an attempted murder case, I'll take this to the D.A. Otherwise, no deal."

"Maybe you should rethink that. I'm also probably the last person to have seen your foster father alive, and it wasn't under the best of circumstances. I was there to take something back, and he caught me."

As she watched, Kim saw Rick's face turn to stone. His jaw was clenched and so were his fists.

"I went to retrieve something for Angelina Tso—now Curley."

"We already know she recorded some of his Sings," Preston said.

"There was more to it than that. Angelina also went through your foster father's stuff and took photos of other things, like the list of Plant People who could harm. He caught her and demanded she erase everything, but she refused. He grabbed the cell phone but couldn't erase the images without knowing her password. He refused to give it back until the photos were erased."

"Why didn't he just take the memory card?" Preston asked.

"Maybe there wasn't one, or he didn't know how to delete the files. Anyway, Angelina hired me to steal the phone back, so I did. The old man caught me, though, and we had a…confrontation. He lost and I took the phone."

"You—" Rick dived toward him, but Preston got in the way and pushed him back. "Not now!"

Rick pulled himself together in an instant. Only the deadly set of his jaw revealed the rage inside him.

"Do you believe Angelina retaliated against Hosteen Silver after that?" Preston asked.

"Yeah. He threw her out, so she couldn't become a medicine woman. Angelina was really pissed off. She didn't think she'd done anything wrong, since she'd paid to learn from him. When you came back home," he said, looking at Rick, "she offered me a new pickup if I got rid of 'the marked man.' She said you were the only one who could connect her with his disappearance. I told her to go fix her own problems."

"You turned her down? Why should I believe that?" Preston asked.

"Taking on one of you amounts to taking on the whole damned family. I'm not afraid of jail, but I'm not stupid," Sandoval said.

"You seem to know a lot, Sandoval," Rick said. "How was my father poisoned?"

"Angelina's niece—Bonnie—likes to talk, so I can make a good guess. Before she became his apprentice, Angelina and Hosteen Silver were friends," he said. "He loved breakfast burritos, and Bonnie sold homemade ones with *naniscaadas*— handmade tortillas. Angelina would deliver some to him every morning when she came for her instruction. One time, after a rain, she got stuck driving through Copper Canyon. I understand you dug her out," he added, looking directly at Rick.

"Was she still bringing Hosteen Silver food at around the time he disappeared? *After* they'd had the falling-out?" Preston queried.

"She wasn't welcome there anymore, so no, but Angelina often helped get the orders ready and it's possible her niece continued with the deliveries to Hosteen Silver."

Rick turned to Preston. "We done here?"

"For now," Preston responded, standing.

"What about me?" Sandoval asked.

"Once we confirm your story, we'll discuss the deal," Preston responded.

They were leaving the room when Rick's cell phone vibrated, indicating a text message.

Rick looked down at the display as Preston closed the door behind them. He showed his brother the message from Detective Bidtah.

"'The substance in the black paint splashed on your windshield is bad news,'" Preston read aloud.

"There's more," Rick said as a new message appeared.

Chapter Nineteen

As soon as they were out in the hall, Rick and Preston met with Paul and Kim. "The paint thrown onto the windshield contained corpse powder, just as I suspected," Rick reported.

"There are some nasty things going on, then," Preston said. "If we want to get to the bottom of it, we're going to have to find Hosteen Silver's body and have it tested for traces of poison. Without it, proving he was murdered will be impossible."

"Let's crash at Daniel's, get some sleep and set out from the ranch house at first light. Each of us will choose a different path to Angelina's old home. We can stay in contact via satellite phone," Rick said, adding, "We'll want Gene on this, too, so we need to get him down here ASAP. That means calling him tonight."

"What about Detective Bidtah?" Paul asked.

"This kind of search isn't tribal police business, not unless we find a body," Preston said. "If we can prove there was a murder, then he has reason to open an investigation."

"It would also be best not to tell anyone outside the family what we're doing," Preston advised. "It'll upset members of our tribe. They'll see what we're doing as dangerous."

"Maybe it is," Rick admitted, "but it's the only shot we've got left."

KIM WOKE UP suddenly to the blast of a coach's whistle. Paul, on the floor a few feet away, sat bolt upright.

"What the—?" Paul growled.

Daniel grinned, holding up the silver sports whistle. "We needed to wake up ready to go, and I thought this would help."

"The aroma of coffee would have been nicer," Kim muttered. She'd insisted on sleeping in one of the sleeping bags just like the others. The only way to be treated as an equal was never to ask for preferential treatment.

She reluctantly scrambled out of the warm bag, then quickly rolled it up and stowed it out of the way, memories of her days in the military flooding back to her.

"We'll have a light breakfast and get under way. Take some of the protein bars and water bottles in the kitchen and put them in your backpacks, too."

Rick stood. "One last thing. We all have to wear

our medicine bags where they can be easily seen. If we need help or if another Navajo sees or guesses what we're doing, we don't want to be mistaken for skinwalkers."

"Good thought," Paul said.

After breakfast, they set out in separate vehicles. Preston rode in his private SUV in case he had to return to Hartley unexpectedly on police business. Daniel and Paul were together in one of their company SUVs.

Once they reached the entrance to Copper Canyon, Daniel would be taking a foot trail toward the site of Angelina's mobile home, joining up with Kyle, who'd meet him on the way. Paul would circle the outside walls of the canyon, looking for undiscovered trails that might have been a possible route if their father had actually continued out of the canyon. Later, he'd join Daniel and Kyle on the other side near the highway.

Gene had decided to take his pickup and drive outside the canyon along the highway, searching for foot trails crossing the main road. Later, he'd join Erin at the ranch house, where they'd act as a control center, coordinating the search and passing along information to the others.

Rick and Kim were to hike to the spot in the canyon where he'd found the notebook, then pass through the secret passage behind the house that led through the cliff walls to the highway. From there, they'd take the quickest route to Angelina's old residence, based on the trails Gene or one of the others discovered.

It was ninety minutes into the plan when Rick and Kim stood beside the highway just west of the hidden passage. Rick consulted a topographic map that Daniel had provided to each of them. "Our trail will take us through that dry canyon I always avoided as a kid," he said as they crossed the highway. They soon entered a wide, shallow arroyo that extended for miles in a sinuous path. "It's that one, on your left," he added, pointing. "This wash narrows up there, and passes right through the gap."

"What bothered you about that place?" she asked, working to keep up with him in the soft ground. The trek, which would require them to walk uphill for at least three miles, was going to be harder than she'd expected.

"This becomes a narrow passage up there between two sandstone cliffs, and the shadowed side is full of caves dug into some of the softer layers of rock. I used to imagine mountain lions or coyotes hiding up there, waiting to pounce."

"A boy's imagination at work," she said with a smile.

"One day I decided to face my fears, so I went up there with a flashlight and a pointed stick—my spear. It was near dusk, and I discovered that some of the shallow caves were habitats for bats. They all came flying out when I stepped inside with my flashlight. I've never been back since."

"They don't come out during this time of day, right?" she asked, not eager to face a dark cloud of bats.

"No, but because this is the quickest route to Angelina's old home, it's probably the path Hosteen Silver took. If I'm right about that, and he found he couldn't make it all the way, he may have sought shelter, hoping to gather his strength. There are some bigger caves up there."

"Makes sense."

They approached a narrow pass flanked by steep hillsides, climbed out of the arroyo, which had narrowed and deepened, then walked along the steep slopes above the dry channel.

"Are those the caves you were talking about?" she asked, pointing up their side of the canyon. "They don't seem so high off the ground."

"You're right. I guess my perspective has changed over the years." He gazed at the caves, lost in thought. "If he was getting weak and the weather was turning bad, my gut tells me he'd have chosen the closest one large enough for a man to crawl into." Rick reached down and touched his medicine pouch. "I'm going in."

"Rick, let me check. This will be easier on me if we find a body. I'm also a lot smaller than you. Hand me the flashlight and I'll take a look."

"No, I have to be there. We can do it together, though," he said, offering his hand. "Let's climb."

The cliff face was by no means vertical, sloping only about forty five degrees, and they didn't need any special gear because of the many handholds and footholds available.

They reached the opening of the shallow cave several minutes later. On their knees at the entrance, he held out his arm, holding her back. "Let's make sure there are no animals inside first."

He brought out his flashlight. "No bats, but there's a stationary figure deep in the shadows."

"I see something back there, too," she whispered.

Angling the flashlight as he leaned forward, resting on his elbows, he finally managed to illuminate the prone shape. He moved the beam around for a few seconds before turning it off.

"Is that him?" Kim asked softly.

"Yes, the heat and the desert appear to have mummified his remains, but that long silver hair and the custom belt buckle tell me all I need to know." His voice was taut.

"He's on his back, like he went to sleep. Would you like me to go over and check for a wallet or something else?" she asked, placing a gentle hand on his arm.

"No. I'll radio my brothers once we're back outside. Once they arrive we'll photograph everything, check the cave for evidence, then put the body in a bag. If the tribe approves, we'll take it to the office of the regional medical investigator in Hartley. Forensic people can check it out. If he was poisoned, then it'll fall to Bidtah to investigate," Rick said, his tone flat and emotionless.

Despite his determination to keep his emotions well under control, she knew he was hurting. Without thinking about it, she threw her arms around him. "I'm so sorry, Rick."

"Searching for his body seems like a betrayal, but if he really was poisoned, letting his murderer go free would have been worse," he said, holding on to her tightly.

"You followed your highest sense of right. He would have expected nothing less from you," she said.

He eased his hold. "I have to let my brothers know," he said, clearing his throat.

Once they were outside the cave, he contacted them. "Make sure we have two sets of gloves for everyone," he added before ending the call. "Not for us but out of respect for him. Hosteen Silver would have wanted it that way."

IT TOOK THEM two hours to get the body into the back of Preston's vehicle.

"Gene, if you can help Preston deliver the remains, I'd like to continue on to where Angelina's mobile home stood at one time and have a look around," Rick said, then glanced at Kim. "You can come with me, or go back to the ranch house and we'll meet there later."

"I'm sticking with you," she said.

"I'll conduct a grid search from the cave where we found the body to see if there's any other physical evidence that'll explain his reasons for coming here," Daniel said. "I'll be in the area, so when you're done, give me a call and I'll either come and get you or meet you someplace."

As Rick and Kim set out, she noticed how quiet he'd become. "Are you okay?"

"I guess."

She took his hand. "You don't always have to be so tough, Rick. We're all human and that means we're all vulnerable," she said gently.

He gave her hand a squeeze. "Right now, you and I have to focus on one thing—life. We're still in danger, so stay alert."

Their route led them away from the canyon and onto a long, downhill slope with low, scattered piñon and juniper trees and waist-high sagebrush. They moved steadily but carefully, on the alert for danger now that the vegetation provided cover for anyone wanting to ambush them.

Soon, they spotted the worn tar-paper roof of a red outbuilding and a flat area cleared of everything but low grass and tumbleweeds. "That's her barn, and to the left is the concrete slab where Angelina's mobile home stood. Let's go take a look around there." He turned and looked back toward the canyon.

"My foster father got within a mile of her trailer before he died," Rick observed. "There's also the possibility that he actually got here, then crawled up into the cave on his way back. Let's see if we can find a lead."

"Like something that belonged to Hosteen Silver, or evidence she overlooked?"

"Exactly."

As they approached, a flock of blackbirds flew up into the sky. He held up his hand and stayed perfectly still, listening.

Kim froze and searched the area, her heart beating as fast as it had when on convoy duty in Afghanistan. Even little clues mattered in life-and-death situations.

Staying behind the cover of a thick juniper, they waited. Then she saw movement and, getting Rick's attention, pointed.

Chapter Twenty

A moment later a coyote come out of the brush with a rabbit in its mouth. The successful hunter then trotted off, quickly disappearing.

"He's found food, so he's not interested in us," Rick said, remaining on alert.

Sensing his uneasiness, she whispered, "What's wrong?"

"I don't know. Maybe it's seeing Coyote, the Trickster. That's how he's known in our legends," he said. "Stay watchful and expect the unexpected."

"All right."

He looked around carefully, then called Daniel. "We're going to move in on the property, but I've got a hunch someone is out there watching. Have you seen anyone, any vehicles?"

"Just a dust trail a while ago along a dirt road east of you. Probably a local. I'll drive over to see if they parked or kept going. It'll take a while for me to get there, so give me a call if you need anything. Be on the lookout for any surprises, like a bear or coyote trap. Whoever is doing this has tried just about everything so far."

"Stay safe," Rick added, ending the call. "All right, then," he said to Kim, "let's move in. Search for footprints or any indication that someone's been by here. Daniel advised us to look for traps, just in case."

He moved forward cautiously, but the birds had come back and all seemed normal as they approached the concrete pad. They circled the area, searching for anything interesting, but only found a few cinder blocks that had probably been used to help level the mobile home.

There were no signs that anyone had been there in quite a while. Cockle burrs, goat-heads and Russian thistle had already appeared in what had been a cleared area. The chain of succession had begun.

"Barns aren't that common out here. Most people have sheep pens," he said, looking over at the dark red building that was about the size of a one-car garage.

"It's old, the paint is fading and the siding is starting to warp. I have a feeling there's not much to see, but let's go take a look inside anyway," Kim suggested.

"Hang on a minute." Rick's gaze took in the area. "I'm getting some bad vibes here." He called Daniel again. "I'm going to check inside the barn," he told his brother after filling him in, "but I want you to call me if it turns out that vehicle ended up heading in this direction. Something still feels off to me."

"Okay. Preston and Gene are on their way to the lab with the remains, but I'll ask Paul to head in this direction. Kyle's monitoring the ranch."

Kim waited till he'd ended the call. "If someone's out there, wouldn't they have done something by now, like shoot at us?" Kim challenged. "They did before."

"If it were me, I'd lay low and wait until the target got real close. Patience can be a reliable weapon."

They went up to the barn doors, but before going inside Rick looked around one more time. Nothing seemed out of place, and there were no footprints, yet the feeling that they were being watched persisted. "We'll take a quick look inside, then walk down the old road leading from here to meet up with my brothers."

They went in just as a gust of cold wind slammed against the side of the barn. The entire building seemed to groan. His uneasiness increased.

"It seems sturdy enough," Kim said, looking around. There were two stalls against one wall, an area with pallets for storing hay, and a crude rack with wooden pegs that held a rake with missing tines and a rusty shovel with a third of the handle gone.

As another hard gust hit the building, the door slammed shut.

"Those gusts are making my skin crawl," she said.

"Wind's said to have power to carry news. Whether it's good or bad, that's for someone else to say."

He studied the wooden walls, full of gaps where the planks had warped and twisted. "At least we don't need the flashlight to find our way around."

The wind had generated a combination of dust and plant debris in the air, and Kim sneezed. "There's nothing in here anymore. Let's leave before my allergies start to kick up," she said.

Rick pushed against the entrance doors, but they refused to yield.

"Is it stuck?" she asked, coming over to give him a hand.

Stepping back, Rick looked through the crack between the barn doors and quickly identified the problem. "The bar that keeps the door shut must have dropped down into place somehow. I'll need something sturdy and slim to slip through the gap and lift it up and out of the way."

"That gap is too narrow for the rake or shovel handle. If we could find a piece of wire, maybe we can wrap it around the bar and lift up."

He sniffed the air. Something else was wrong. "Do you smell it?"

"Dust and moldy hay that's making me sneeze. Is that what you mean?"

He glanced around in the dimly lit interior and by the time he brought the flashlight from his backpack, smoke was visible against the north wall.

"Someone set the outside of the barn on fire." He tossed her the phone. "Get Dan. We need him here in a hurry. I'll grab the shovel and try to lift the bar using the blade."

Through the gaps between the boards, he could see the stack of dead tumbleweeds piled up against the side of the barn. Each ignited one after the other into white smoke and flame.

Kim made the call, then ran over to Rick. "Daniel's on his way, but it'll take him several minutes to get here."

Rick picked up the shovel, but the blade was curved like a scoop. He tried to make it work, but there was no way he could angle it through the opening to raise the bar.

As he turned his head to check the progress of the fire, smoke was flowing up the wall, entering through the gaps between the boards. Flames were visible in places and the tumbleweeds burning outside crackled loudly as they were consumed.

"Daniel won't get here in time, will he?" she asked, her voice shaky.

He didn't answer. "Look for a weak spot in the wall. I'm going to make our own door."

Kim coughed as the white smoke became thicker and the sharp scent of burning wood began to penetrate her lungs.

"Put something over your nose and mouth, or pull up your shirt and breathe through the fabric," Rick directed, leaning against the wall, looking for a place to smash through.

"This is a weak point," Rick said. "Some of the planks are split." Using the blade of the shovel as a spear, he began to work. After the third jab, the plank broke in two, leaving an eight-inch, waist-high gap.

The next plank was tougher, but in four jabs he'd knocked it loose from the uprights and it fell to the ground outside.

"One more plank and we can crawl out," she yelled, her voice raspy now as she gasped for air.

The wind and smoke picked up quickly, intensifying the fire, which was crackling louder than ever.

Coughing, he pulled Kim to her knees close to the hole he'd made in the side of the barn.

There was a loud whoosh across the barn. The opposite wall was a sheet of flames leading from floor to roof. "We've got to get out of here *now!*"

He dropped the shovel, lowered his shoulder and charged the gap he'd made in the side.

The building shook as he hit the wall, and several planks snapped from the impact as he broke out into the open, nearly falling to the ground.

Turning his head, he saw Kim stumble out through the gap. Catching her with both arms, he brought her up against him.

"We're okay now," he reassured her, kissing her forehead tenderly.

Hearing running footsteps, Rick pushed her behind him and aimed his gun at the far corner of the barn. Had the firebug come back to finish them off?

As Paul and Daniel came into view, Rick lowered his weapon.

"Easy, bro," Daniel said. "We're the good guys."

DETECTIVE BIDTAH ARRIVED a half hour later, finding them quickly thanks to the black smoke rising from the smoldering wreckage of the barn. He was not happy to see them, judging from the first words he spoke after climbing out of his SUV. "You're investigating on *my* turf but you didn't call me till now?"

"We weren't sure this was a police matter, so we gave you plausible deniability," Rick said. He quickly explained that the purpose of the removal of Hosteen Silver's body was to try to determine the cause of death.

"If the death proves suspicious, it's my case," Bidtah reminded him. "Now tell me more about you and Ms. Nelson being locked inside this barn."

"Here's how it went down," Rick said, then explained.

"There are lots of footprints around," Bidtah said after Rick had finished. "At a guess, I'd say most belong to you two or your brothers," he added, looking at their boots. "There's a strong scent of charcoal lighter here, too. That must be what the arsonist used to ignite the tumbleweeds."

Rick nodded. "I can smell it now."

"Any of you find anything else I can use?" Bidtah asked, looking from Kim to the brothers.

They shook their heads. "The cave where we found the body is about fifty feet up the south wall of the canyon," Rick told him. "You'll be able to spot it from our tracks."

"Not looking forward to it," Bidtah said. "Your dad was a good man. You let me know as soon as you hear from the lab," Bidtah ordered. "And email me all the photos you took of the scene."

"Absolutely," Rick replied.

"The murder of a highly regarded medicine man is going to send ripples through our community," Bidtah said, rubbing his chin pensively.

"Probably, but it'll be up to you to determine

how much you want to divulge to the public," Rick noted.

"It's hard to keep secrets on the Rez," the detective commented.

Rick nodded slowly. "I know."

Bidtah glanced over to where the mobile home had once stood. "I'll have to speak to Angelina Curley as soon as possible. Like your place, this land belongs to the tribe, and if she's not occupying it, the land should go to another Navajo family," Bidtah said. "I also intend to ask why she chose to move away. If she was running from something, I want to know."

THEY WERE BACK at Daniel's a short while later, but a somber mood had settled over them.

"How soon will we hear from the medical investigator?" Kyle asked.

"That depends," Preston answered. "All they've got to work with is hair, bones, bone marrow and a few viable tissue samples. Jack's given it top priority, however."

"While we wait for results, we need to find out more about Angelina's niece and her homemade burritos," Rick said. "That's the only possible vector for the poison we know about right now."

Paul, who was at the computer, spoke up. "The woman's name is Bonnie Herder. She's a single mom with three kids. She owns her own small business, has a catering truck and usually parks by the public high school in Shiprock."

"School lets out in less than an hour. I'm going to go talk to her," Rick declared.

"I can't question her because she's out of my jurisdiction," Preston said. "If I try, I'm going to stir up a real hornet's nest. The way things stand, Bidtah would take it as an affront."

"You shouldn't go, either, Rick, because she's bound to know exactly who you are," Kyle said.

"Let me talk to her," Kim offered. "I'll just pretend I'm a substitute teacher on a break. I'll get further if it doesn't look like an interrogation."

"Kim just might get away with that," Preston agreed with a nod. "But you'll need to stay out of sight, Rick, or you'll blow it for her."

"I'm not happy with this plan," Rick said.

"Why?" Kim countered. "I can handle this. By keeping it friendly, we may get the information we need without her realizing it could be a problem for her aunt."

"I agree with Kim," Daniel said.

Rick shook his head. "We're after a killer. Kim will be unarmed as well, so she runs double the risk."

"Not if you're close by, backing her up," Preston said. "She's not likely to get violent that close to so many potential witnesses anyway."

TWENTY MINUTES LATER, wearing a change of clothes so she wouldn't smell like smoke, Rick and Kim set out in one of Level One's SUVs.

"Have you ever met Bonnie?" she asked him.

"Not that I recall. But a single mother with three kids and a business has a lot to lose. If she knows anything or if she's involved, she'll be on her guard. Be careful how you ask your questions and don't target Angelina specifically. Find out if Bonnie's family helps her prepare the food or if she has regular helpers, and so on."

"I've got this, trust me," she said.

"I do, but I still hate having you take point."

"You won't be far. Why are you worried?"

He kept his gaze focused on the road ahead. "You're more important to me than anything else, including this case. Do you understand me?"

"No. Are you saying that you think I can't handle this or that you're afraid you can't?" she added with a tiny smile.

"Maybe both. I love you, Kim," he said. Pulling over onto the side of the road, he hauled her into his arms.

Before she had the chance to react, he kissed her hard, moving his mouth over hers until her lips parted.

He was rough, desperate for more, but with a groan, released her. "No matter what happens, I'll have your back," he said, putting the SUV back in gear.

Dazed, happy, her heart pounding overtime in her ears, she nodded, not trusting her voice. He loved her! He'd shown her in countless ways and now he'd actually said the words.

She smiled. No matter what happened from this point on, she'd always have this.

Chapter Twenty-One

"I shouldn't have told you that, Kim, not right now," he said, cutting into her thoughts less than a mile later. "We have to focus on one thing—survival."

"But I feel the same way about you, Rick. I—"

"No. Don't say anything else, not until the danger's past. Do this for me. For us."

She wasn't sure if he thought he'd change his mind after the dust cleared or whether he thought she might. Either way, she wouldn't press him. Trying to hide her disappointment, she nodded. "Okay."

Twenty minutes later they reached the high school south of the main highway. "School hasn't let out yet, so she probably won't be surrounded by students," he said, passing by without slowing. "There's the catering truck parked just down the road."

"Good. That'll make my work easier," Kim said, not looking directly as they passed the truck, which now had the sliding panel up and counter out, ready for customers.

"Listen to me carefully, Kim. If you sense trouble, cut it short and head back to the SUV."

"Sure, but remember I'm not going to confront her. I'm going to talk to her—one working woman to another."

"All right. I'll park here, out of sight." He turned into a big empty lot a few hundred yards farther down.

Kim took a deep breath, smiled and went up to the catering truck's window. "I'm starving. What do you have that I can eat fast?"

The young woman smiled. "Lucky you're going to just beat the after-school rush."

"Which means I've got to hurry. What can you recommend?" Kim asked.

"My bestseller is the green chili burger on homemade tortillas."

"Sounds good. I'll have one," she said. "Mild."

As the woman assembled the burger, Kim introduced herself.

"I'm Bonnie," the woman answered. "You're new around here, aren't you?"

"At this high school here, yes. I'm substituting today. But I grew up in Hartley."

"Half an hour drive. That's not too bad," Bonnie said.

Kim rubbed the back of her neck with one hand and made sure the woman saw the gesture. "I've been sitting at the desk way too long. Time for stretching exercises. I just wish I could find something to ease the sore muscles. The over-the-counter pills give me stomach problems and the ointments smell like a locker room."

"Have you considered herbs? Our medicine men are very knowledgeable about things like that."

"That's what I've heard. Can you recommend someone?"

"No, not really. The one I knew isn't around anymore," she said, placing the snack-size burger in a small microwave oven as she spoke.

"My friend got a cream from a local medicine man, Mr....something. Ruby swore by it, but I can't remember the man's name."

"Hosteen Silver?" Bonnie asked. Seeing Kim nod, she smiled sadly and continued. "He was really nice, and a great healer. My aunt would take him some of my freshly made breakfast burritos every morning. She was his apprentice for a time." Bonnie took the warmed burger out of the microwave and placed it on the counter.

"Your aunt is a medicine woman?" Kim asked, paying for the food.

"No, she didn't want to spend half her life in training. She got married instead."

"This burger's excellent," Kim said after taking

a bite. "When the kids are out, like for lunch, I'm sure business is nonstop. Do you have any helpers?"

"My aunt used to help me get the *naniscaadas* ready each morning, but now she has her own business."

Hearing a bell, Kim turned toward the high school's main building. "I better get back to my room before I get run down by the fleeing kids," Kim said.

She left quickly and within a minute was surrounded by teens hurrying toward the food truck. Kim reversed course and walked back to the SUV, this time passing behind the food truck and staying out of view.

She ate the last bite as she slipped inside the SUV. "Now we have confirmation that Sandoval was telling the truth. Angelina used to help Bonnie make the *naniscaada,* then would take freshly made breakfast burritos over to your foster father every morning."

"Let me call Preston. This doesn't constitute proof, but it's something to work from."

Preston answered on the first ring and Rick put his phone on speaker. "I'm at the medical investigator's lab now," Preston announced. "The preliminary tests run on tissue samples drew a blank. One of the lab techs found a dried leaf in his shirt pocket, however. At first it looked like parsley, but the botanist recognized it as *Aethusa cynapium,* known commonly as fool's parsley or, get this, garden hemlock."

"Hemlock is deadly, remember Socrates?" Kim commented.

"Exactly," Preston responded. "According to what I was told, death can take anywhere from hours to days. If that's what killed him, Hosteen Silver might have known what was coming. The problem is that it's hard to prove it is the cause of death, because the only postmortem sign of hemlock is asphyxia. That can't be established, not now."

"That leaf didn't end up in his pocket by accident. In his last hours he must have suspected the source and kept that leaf for someone—maybe us—to find," Rick said.

"Problem is, we can't prove who put that poison in his food, or even if that's what killed him," Preston pointed out.

"If you come up with any ideas, let me know. I'll do the same." Rick ended the call.

Pulling to the side of the road, Rick stopped the SUV and turned to look at Kim. "Looks like we have to force the issue. Angelina's easily angered, so I think it's time to push her and see what happens."

"I agree. Today's Friday, her day to go see two silversmiths who live up by Teec Nos Pos, just inside the Arizona state line. The drive usually stresses her out, but she's always insisted on going herself. The woman doesn't trust anyone else to bargain hard enough. If we catch her on the road, I'm willing to bet it won't take much to rattle her."

He considered it. "I'm going to bluff her out to see if I can make her blink first," he said. "Any idea where these silversmiths live?"

"Yes. Angelina kept a map in the store so we could track her down if she got stuck in bad weather or had car trouble. She takes the northwest road out of Shiprock to Teec Nos Pos, turns south at mile marker twenty-nine just past the local Chapter House, then continues on a dirt road into the foothills for about five miles. The silversmiths are father and son, but she has to deal with them separately."

Rick called his brothers and asked them to meet him at mile marker twenty-nine.

RICK AND KIM were already halfway there, so they arrived first and pulled off the main highway, positioning the vehicle so they could see anyone coming their way up the dirt road. Daniel, Paul and Preston would be delayed by a half hour.

"She normally arrives back at the store before six, and it's about fifty-five miles from here. If her business is done, she should be passing through here before long."

After ten minutes she pointed. "That looks like her pickup coming in our direction."

"All right then." Rick pulled out and blocked the road.

A minute later the truck was close enough for them to confirm who was driving. Angelina honked the horn, slowed and finally stopped about fifteen feet up the road.

She climbed out, a thirty-thirty Winchester rifle in her hand. "What's going on here?"

Rick got out and walked over to the front of the vehicle. "Remember me?"

"Like a disease. When you're around, nothing good ever happens. Get out of my way."

Rick took a breath, determined to keep his cool. "I need to talk to you. It's important."

"Forget it. I'm not interested."

"You better be, because the Navajo police are on their way here as we speak," he answered, lying through his teeth.

Angelina watched Kim as she came out the driver's side and walked over to stand beside Rick. "You traitor."

Kim said nothing and Angelina kept her rifle in front of her, not aiming at the moment.

"You'll be interested to know we found my foster father's body," he said. "It was up in one of those caves, easy walking distance from where you used to live in that mobile home. Did he die on the way there or on the way back? Tell me."

Angelina's eyes widened slightly, then settled down. "After nearly three years, you finally went looking for that old fool?" She shuddered. "How do you know it was even him?"

"There was no mistaking his clothing, his belt and, of course, his hair. That remains long after death when preserved in a dry cave," he said. "But here's where it gets interesting, Angelina. His final act was to scratch out your name on the wall of the cave."

Her eyes narrowed for a second. She cleared her throat. "He had a thing for me. I must have been the last person he thought of before he died."

"No, he was poisoned and the police think he did that to name his killer. He also kept a leaf in his pocket. A leaf of fool's parsley—garden hemlock. Where'd you get that anyway? Grow it on a windowsill, maybe?"

Angelina stood rock-still, but her right index finger inched toward the rifle's trigger.

"And we know how you delivered the fatal dose, too," Kim added. "You brought food from Bonnie's truck out to Hosteen Silver every morning. You helped her fix them, as a matter of fact. A little extra chili on it...and something that looked like parsley. He never even noticed until it was too late."

"He taught you all about plants, and you used that against him," Rick snarled. "Before the police get here, at least tell me why you killed him. That's the only part I still don't get."

Angelina levered a shell into the rifle chamber. "If only you'd just run off that cliff…"

"Don't get stupid, Angelina. If you shoot us, any chance you have will go right out the window. We're standing in Arizona now, and they have the death penalty."

He pointed down the road toward the west. A white sedan was heading their way. "There's the Arizona highway patrol right now." He was bluffing.

As Angelina swung the rifle barrel around, Rick dove behind the engine compartment, pushing Kim down ahead of him. "Stay low," he yelled, rolling up into a crouch.

Angelina fired, the bullet ricocheting off the reinforced hood.

Rick poked his head out around the front bumper and ducked back as she fired again, shattering the front headlight inches from his head.

Rick reached down for his pistol, but his holster was empty. Glancing around, he spotted the pistol lying in the sand a few feet away. It must have slipped out when he'd dived to the ground. He lunged for it just as Angelina jumped into her pickup.

As he brought the pistol up, shaking sand from the barrel, Angelina sped by Rick's vehicle on the passenger side, sideswiping the SUV with a teeth-shattering screech.

Rick, on one knee, spun around, aimed carefully and fired two rounds into the rear of her truck as it reached the highway.

"She's getting away," Kim yelled, racing around to the passenger side as Angelina sped east toward Teec Nos Pos.

Rick jumped in and handed her his pistol. Whipping the vehicle around, he pulled onto the road right behind a frightened-looking elderly couple in a white sedan. They were clearly not Arizona Highway Patrol officers.

As they accelerated after the fleeing silver pickup, Rick looked over at Kim. "You okay?"

She looked down at her right hand, which was on her lap on top of his pistol. "Scrapes and stickers, but mostly I'm angry."

"Me, too."

His phone rang, and with a flick of his finger, he put it on speaker, keeping both hands on the wheel. Doing eighty, Rick whipped around the white sedan as if it was standing still.

"Hey, Rick, where are you?" It was Preston's voice. "A silver pickup almost ran us off the road. Was that—?"

"Angelina," Rick confirmed. "We're coming up fast. Once we pass you, turn around and give chase."

"Copy. I see you now."

Kim signaled the men as they raced past Rick's brothers at ninety miles per hour.

"You're flying, bro, slow down." Preston's voice came over the phone instantly.

"Can't. Unless I keep her in sight, she could pull off anywhere."

"She won't get far. I see a trail of fluid on the road. I'm guessing she's losing gas," Preston told him.

Kim looked down at the road ahead. "I see the shine on the asphalt."

Rick slowed to eighty-five. "Okay. I'm slowing down. I have the truck within sight now."

"Her new home isn't far from here, a few miles past Beclabito, on the right," Kim advised, referring to the small community ahead, just inside the New Mexico state line.

Rick nodded. "Hear what Kim said, guys?"

"Copy," Preston acknowledged. "Once you confirm her route, let us know. We're about a mile behind you now."

About three minutes later, the Beclabito trading post fading in the rearview mirror, Kim pointed toward a cloud of dust ahead, to the right of the highway. "That's the turnoff. Did she wreck?"

Rick took a long look and spotted a vehicle

emerging from the right side of the cloud. "No, she may have spun out, though. She's headed home, guys," he said loud enough for Preston to hear over the speaker.

A minute later Rick turned, pointing to skid marks on the asphalt and road shoulder. "Look at those ruts. She nearly lost it making the turn."

"Her home is a few miles ahead, just on other side of those cliffs, up against a hill," Kim reported. "With that rifle, she might be planning to ambush us when we go through the road cut."

Rick slowed, noting the trail of damp earth in the center of the dirt road. "Still losing gas. Once she runs out, we've got her."

They topped a small rise and saw the pickup in the middle of the road about two hundred yards ahead. Steep cliffs rose on both sides of the road cut. "How many rounds did she fire from that Winchester?" Kim asked.

"Three, maybe four. Her rifle holds six to seven rounds normally, so she's still armed and dangerous. With that weapon she also has a range advantage and hitting power over our pistols."

"We need to play it smart," Kim said. "Make her waste her ammo."

Rick slowed to a crawl, then turned, blocking the road. "My feelings exactly. Follow me out on my side. Once the guys arrive we can move in. They'll cover us."

"Assault tactics."

"Exactly, except they won't open up unless Angelina actually starts shooting," he said. "We'll advance along both drainage ditches. Stay low and be ready to go prone if she opens fire."

Preston, already briefed on the tactical plan, pulled up behind them. With backup now in place, Rick and Kim moved ahead to the silver vehicle. The smell of gasoline was thick in the air.

Rick looked around. "Her footprints don't lead down the road toward the house. They lead off to the right. I can still track her."

"Maybe she's just circling around, hoping to lose us by climbing up some trail to the top of the mesa. Once she's up there, she could shoot down on us," Kim said.

"If she wanted to make a last stand, yes, but I don't think she wants a fight, Kim. I think she's looking to hide. She'll head someplace she feels safe."

He stood back from the cliff, looking along the upper third of the formation. Feeling the vibration on his cell phone, he brought his brothers up to speed. "There are shallow caves up there. My guess is she made it to one of those. Someone needs to keep watch for a rifle barrel poking out. Once we start our climb, she'll have to poke her head out to shoot at us."

"We'll provide suppressive fire if she shows herself," Preston replied.

Rick put the phone in his pocket and glanced over at Kim. "From this point on we'll have to be as silent as possible."

"All right. Let's go."

Pushing some dried tumbleweeds out of the way, they worked their way up. This slope was a lot easier to climb than the cliff where they'd found Hosteen Silver's remains.

The first few caves were nothing more than low overhangs and were easy to see inside. He moved past them, signaling for Kim to remain in place. He then headed alone toward what looked like a deep cave.

He immediately found a small path and shoe prints. Angelina had come this way.

He glanced back and, spotting his brothers below, pointed ahead. He then signaled Kim to follow him.

As Rick got closer to the cave, he saw what looked like the barrel of a rifle lying on the floor of the cave. He motioned for Kim to hold her ground, then carefully advanced to a position beside the opening.

From where he stood, he could see that the lever of the rifle was half-open, a bent cartridge in the breech. A jam, probably caused in panic by an inexperienced shooter. Reaching over, he grabbed the barrel, pulled out the rifle and slid it down the slope. It hung up on some brush about fifteen feet from the opening.

Rick pulled a wide-beamed flashlight out of his pocket and examined the cave from outside. It was much bigger than the one he'd been in earlier that day, about five feet high toward the rear, maybe ten feet wide, and at least double that distance deep. At the back were what appeared to be two shrines.

Rick entered on his knees, rose to a crouch and discovered a pair of snapshots hanging on the rock wall above two sets of personal effects.

He recognized Hosteen Silver's photo first. Beneath it, on the floor of the cave, were his foster father's favorite jeans—an old pair with worn knees and a paint stain—and his bolo tie.

He focused the beam of the flashlight on the other photo. It was a photo showing Angelina in a wedding dress standing beside a man in a suit. That suit appeared to have been folded and placed below the photo, along with a gold wedding band.

Hearing a muted sound, he turned his head to see Kim crouched at the entrance.

"What is this place, a memorial?" Kim whispered, coming up beside him.

"Of a sort, I guess," he answered in a quiet voice. As he looked into the darkness, he spotted a small flicker of light, like that from a cigarette lighter, followed by the soft glow of a newly lit candle.

The jar candle was on a large wooden box and beside it was Angelina, sitting on a low, three-legged stool. She was holding a shiny steel pistol in a shaky hand, the barrel aimed right at them. "You shouldn't have followed me here. This is my place—and theirs. We can be together here."

For a moment Rick had no words. Then he saw the basketball-size propane bottle beside the box, only a few feet from Angelina.

"You must miss them terribly," Kim said, backing away slightly.

"They never really loved me, but here we're together."

"Angelina, put the pistol down and come outside with us," Rick said. "More violence isn't going to solve anything."

"Don't worry. We won't suffer. We'll all disappear in a big ball of light. I can't miss." She shifted, aiming the pistol at the valve on top of the propane bottle.

The woman was clearly not in her right mind. One shot would destroy the valve, the propane would escape and the candle would ignite the gas, blowing them to bits.

"It's time for me to join my men. This wasn't supposed to include you, too, but Hosteen Silver will appreciate the company."

Seeing her finger tighten around the trigger, Rick grabbed Kim's hand and yanked her to the ground. The pistol went off with an ear-shattering blast. The metal propane tank passed over their heads like a low-flying jet, bounced off the roof of the cave and disappeared out the opening.

Rick turned and saw Angelina on her side, staring at the candle, extinguished by the rush of air and gas. Dust began to shower down, followed by rocks and big chunks of sandstone.

"Out! Everything's coming down," he yelled, wrapping his arm around Kim and pulling her out of the cave.

They leaped out headfirst and slid down the steep slope several feet before he finally managed to grab a ledge with his free hand and stop their slide.

A faint scream somewhere above them was followed by a loud crash as the cave collapsed under the weight of the cliff above. The earth shook and clouds of dust shot out. Big chunks of rock came tumbling down.

Rick pulled Kim to his side, shielding her with his body as loose earth, plant debris and sandstone chunks pelted them.

They waited, heads buried beneath their arms until the earth stopped shaking. An enormous slab of sandstone directly overhead was teetering back and forth.

"Let's move!"

They half slid, half crawled to the bottom,

scrambling to their feet just as there was a final, enormous thud. The sandstone slab tipped, crashed onto the steep slope, then slid halfway down before coming to a stop in a cloud of dust.

Kim couldn't stop shaking. "I thought we were done for," she said, her voice breaking.

Rick pulled her into his arms. "Me, too, and all the time we were stuck there, all I could think of was how much time I'd wasted."

He cupped her face in his hands and kissed her. "I love you, Kim. Marry me."

"Yes!"

They heard footsteps and broke apart to find his brothers standing there.

Daniel laughed. "Jeez, guy, you're covered in dust and dirt, weeds and stickers in your hair—basically you look like a pistol-packing lizard that just crawled out of an ant bed. Where's the romance? Couldn't you have waited for wine and roses, or at least gotten down on one knee?"

"We'll do the rest later, but I'm not wasting one more minute," Rick replied, kissing her again.

"Quit goofing off, slacker," Preston yelled from farther down. "We've still got work to do here."

"Hey, don't ruin the moment," Daniel yelled back.

Rick looked down at Kim, then pointed. "Look at Copper Canyon, off in the distance. No matter what happens, it continues to stand. That's the way it'll be with us."

"I know," she said and kissed him. "Some things were just meant to be."

Epilogue

A week had passed, and with all the major questions answered now, there was no reason not to resume their personal lives again.

Rick had wanted to keep their wedding simple, with only a justice of the peace, his brothers and their families present, including Kim's uncle Frank. The event, scheduled to begin in forty-five minutes, would be the first held at Copper Canyon.

While the women got ready in the next room, Rick stared at Hosteen Silver's journal. With all of them present, they'd read it at first light that morning.

"That's an amazingly detailed history of all the sacred objects he used for each Sing," Rick said. "It's a very special kind of family history."

"None of us will become medicine men, but this kind of knowledge should be preserved," Kyle said.

"Let's keep it safe and secure for the next generation," Preston suggested. "Think of the journal as Hosteen Silver's legacy."

"I like that," Paul said with a nod. "Who's to say one of our children won't become a medicine man or woman?"

Daniel's phone buzzed, signaling a text message. "It's the justice of the peace. He's running ahead of schedule."

Paul went down the hall and knocked on the closed door. "The judge is going to be early. Fifteen minutes. You ladies okay with that?"

A moment later Kim came out and Rick moved to where she stood. "You look beautiful."

She looked down at her dark silk slacks and lacy cream blouse. "I'm ready," she said, running her fingers through her hair.

"It's not too late to change your mind if you want a fancier wedding."

"No. This place made you the man you are, and everyone who counts in our lives is here, including my new family. I couldn't ask for more. It's perfect."

Excitement was thick in the air as they gathered outside. It was truly an Indian summer at the moment. The October sun was high in the sky, it was almost seventy degrees and today the canyon was unusually silent. It was almost as if it were holding its breath.

A gentle breeze blew past them as they stood beside the tallest pine, a tiny blue feather from a piñon jay floated by. She caught it in her hand. "Look! How beautiful!"

Rick looked down at it, amazed. "Hosteen Silver had one he carried in his medicine pouch. It's a symbol of peace and happiness—a powerful omen."

"You told me once that the good in him is part of Universal Harmony, so in a way, he's here with you today."

"I think so, too," Rick murmured, lifting her hand to his lips and kissing it gently.

The justice of the peace arrived. Climbing down from his oversize pickup, he joined the gathering. "We all here? Everyone ready?"

Seeing Rick nod, he opened a small book and began. "Dearly beloved…"

Memories were made one day at a time, and as Rick looked at his bride, he knew today was just the beginning.

* * * * *

LARGER-PRINT BOOKS!

HARLEQUIN *Presents*

PASSION GUARANTEED SEDUCTION

GET 2 FREE LARGER-PRINT
NOVELS PLUS 2 FREE GIFTS!

LARGER-PRINT BOOKS!
GET 2 FREE LARGER-PRINT NOVELS PLUS
2 FREE GIFTS!

HARLEQUIN®

Romance

From the Heart, For the Heart

LARGER-PRINT BOOKS!
GET 2 FREE LARGER-PRINT NOVELS PLUS
2 FREE GIFTS!

HARLEQUIN

super romance®

More Story...More Romance

YES! Please send me 2 FREE LARGER-PRINT Harlequin® Superromance® novels and my 2 FREE gifts (gifts are worth about $10). After receiving them, if I don't wish to receive any more books, I can return the shipping statement marked "cancel." If I don't cancel, I will receive 6 brand-new novels every month and be billed just $5.69 per book in the U.S. or $5.99 per book in Canada. That's a savings of at least 16% off the cover price! It's quite a bargain! Shipping and handling is just 50¢ per book in the U.S. or 75¢ per book in Canada.* I understand that accepting the 2 free books and gifts places me under no obligation to buy anything. I can always return a shipment and cancel at any time. Even if I never buy another book, the two free books and gifts are mine to keep forever.

139/339 HDN F46Y

Name _____ (PLEASE PRINT)

Address _____ Apt. #

City _____ State/Prov. _____ Zip/Postal Code

Signature (if under 18, a parent or guardian must sign)

Mail to the **Harlequin®** Reader Service:
IN U.S.A.: P.O. Box 1867, Buffalo, NY 14240-1867
IN CANADA: P.O. Box 609, Fort Erie, Ontario L2A 5X3

Are you a current subscriber to Harlequin Superromance books and want to receive the larger-print edition?
Call 1-800-873-8635 today or visit www.ReaderService.com.

* Terms and prices subject to change without notice. Prices do not include applicable taxes. Sales tax applicable in N.Y. Canadian residents will be charged applicable taxes. Offer not valid in Quebec. This offer is limited to one order per household. Not valid for current subscribers to Harlequin Superromance Larger-Print books. All orders subject to credit approval. Credit or debit balances in a customer's account(s) may be offset by any other outstanding balance owed by or to the customer. Please allow 4 to 6 weeks for delivery. Offer available while quantities last.

Your Privacy—The Harlequin® Reader Service is committed to protecting your privacy. Our Privacy Policy is available online at www.ReaderService.com or upon request from the Harlequin Reader Service.

We make a portion of our mailing list available to reputable third parties that offer products we believe may interest you. If you prefer that we not exchange your name with third parties, or if you wish to clarify or modify your communication preferences, please visit us at www.ReaderService.com/consumerschoice or write to us at Harlequin Reader Service Preference Service, P.O. Box 9062, Buffalo, NY 14269. Include your complete name and address.

Reader Service.com

Manage your account online!

- Review your order history
- Manage your payments
- Update your address

> ### *We've designed the Harlequin® Reader Service website just for you.*

Enjoy all the features!

- Reader excerpts from any series
- Respond to mailings and special monthly offers
- Discover new series available to you
- Browse the Bonus Bucks catalog
- Share your feedback